SHOW ME YOUR ROCKY MOUNTAINS!

SHOW ME YOUR ROCKY MOUNTAINS!

Thelma Hatch Wyss

Deseret Book Company
Salt Lake City, Utah

For my son, David

Library of Congress Cataloging in Publication Data

Wyss, Thelma Hatch.
  Show me your Rocky Mountains!

  Summary: A twelve-year-old collier leaves
England in 1856 with his mother and brother and
travels by chartered ship across the Atlantic
and by train and handcart across America to the
Promised Land of the Mormons.
  [1. Voyages and travels—Fiction.
2. Mormons—Fiction. 3. Church of Jesus Christ
of Latter-day Saints—Fiction] I. Title.
PZ7.W998Sh 1982   [Fic]   82-9471
 ISBN 0-87747-920-8   AACR2

*And it shall come to pass in the last
days, that the mountain of the Lord's house
shall be established in the top of
the mountains, and shall be exalted
above the hills; and all nations
shall flow unto it.*

(Isaiah 2:2.)

Contents

Acknowledgments

Many individuals and institutions have been helpful in the writing of this book. I give thanks to the Genealogical Library and the Historical Department of The Church of Jesus Christ of Latter-day Saints, the Utah State Historical Society, and the State Historical Society of Iowa.

I am especially grateful for help and hospitality to Mr. and Mrs. Walter Whittamore and Mrs. E. Gibbs of the Historical Society of Eastwood, England.

For histories of their families I express gratitude to Mrs. Ann S. Herrick of Twin Falls, Idaho, a granddaughter of Hannah Rachel Stones, and to Mrs. Ethel T. Page of Payson, Utah, a daughter of Jesse Taylor.

T.H.W.

I
One of a City, and Two of a Family

1

Even before the knocker rapped at the downstairs window, William was awake. He always awakened to neighbor Rowland's call on the left and then lay waiting for his grandfather's summons.

"Henry Soar! Up and to work, my good man, hinny!"

William often wondered who woke up to Grandfather Soar's call, because there was no neighbor on the right.

Grandfather Soar lived at No. 3 Engine Lane in Beggarley Bottom, the first house in the long row of sixteen red brick houses with black slate roofs. At the east end of the row was a larger brick house for the Superior, and at the end of Engine Lane, across the railway line, was the colliery.

It was the green steam engine puffing back and forth along this line carrying coal from Moorgreen Colliery to the Erewash Canal that gave Engine Lane its name.

For as long as old folks could remember, the lane had been an ancient horse and bridle road following along Beggarley Brook, leading from the hamlet of Beggarley in the meadows to the market town of Eastwood on the hill.

Many years ago a Saxon clan had lived along Beggarley Brook, building their wattle and daub dwellings, picking berries in the meadows, and hunting in nearby Sherwood

Forest. Then the fearless Normans came and made their huts along the lane, tilling the land to pay homage to their Lord of Nottingham.

In 1830 when the Barber and Walker Company sank one of its six deep mines at the end of the road, laid the railway line, and built the row of brick houses on the left, the road became known as Engine Lane. It had been Engine Lane, black with coal dust, as long as William could remember, and eleven years seemed like a long time.

William once asked Grandfather Soar if all the beggars in the land came to Beggarley Bottom. Grandfather Soar laughed and said that from the beginning of time this meadowland at the bottom of the hill was the place of the *begers*—the best wild berries in all England.

William also asked Grandfather Soar who woke up the knocker. And Grandfather Soar said, "God Himself, Willy. God Himself."

William was wide awake this autumn morning in 1855, but he lay still, listening. He could hear the old knocker passing through the gate, shuffling in his heavy boots down the lane. Wiliam knew it would not take long for him to reach the next row of houses on Greenhills Road, six old cottages with their thatched roofs falling in. Then turning south to the seven rows of brick houses in the Breach, he would wake up Uncle John Clifford.

After that, William did not know where the old knocker went, but he knew that soon Uncle John and a throng of other colliers would come trooping down Engine Lane, swinging their flickering lamps, appearing like ghosts out of the powdered mist.

And his mother, as always, would call from the gate. "That you, John? Mind you, watch out for my boys in the pit!"

Soon all the colliers in Beggarley Bottom would be up and ready to work. Soon all of Eastwood would be up and ready to work at their mining and farming and framework knitting—ready to work for Squire Barber and Squire Walker, industrial magnates.

Grandfather Soar rolled over in his bed. "Awake, my boys?"

The boys were awake. They had been awake since the knocker called for neighbor Rowland.

Henry in the same bed with Grandfather Soar mumbled, "Aye, Pa."

And in the other bed, William and his ten-year-old brother, Jesse, both answered, "Aye, Grandpa."

But they did not stir, not until they heard their mother, Mary, rattling the coals in the fireplace downstairs.

Grandfather Soar left for work first, wearing the baggy trousers and loose smock of a farm laborer, his lunch in a snap bag slung over his shoulder. Outside at the gate he met his oldest son, Thomas, and together they walked across the meadows to the cabbage fields at Coney Gray Farm.

The three boys dressed by the fire, tugging at their heavy moleskin trousers and leather boots still damp from yesterday's work. Then they pulled on their flannel vests, big jackets, and round leather caps, hurriedly wrapped thin woolen scarves around their necks, and tucked snap bags and tin bottles into their big pockets. They were ready just in time, for they could hear the parade of colliers tramping down Engine Lane, singing.

Out of the gray mist a tall figure loomed over the gate.

"That you, John?" Mary peered up into the face of a husky, bearded collier. "Mind you, take care of my boys!"

Uncle John nodded.

5

And William, Jesse, and Henry joined the singing colliers on their way to Moorgreen Colliery.

> *'Tis I make the ladies and gentlemen warm,*
> *Tho' I haven't no Latin nor learning.*
> *Tho' I get 'em their coals for winter and storm*
> *They don't think of me while they're burning.*
>
> *I squat in the dark to give them their light,*
> *And I hew while they are in slumber.*
> *Tho' I don't think it rhyme, or reason, or right,*
> *I shouldn't be one of their number.*

For twelve hours the boys crawled through the dark, wet tunnels of Moorgreen coal mine. And that evening when they shuffled back down Engine Lane with Uncle John, they were too tired to sing.

Every night Mary scrubbed the boys in turn in a wooden tub on the hearth rug, scrubbing harder each year as if rubbing out the last words of her husband. "Keep the lads out of the pit, Mary," he'd said.

After the scrubbing and a supper of boiled cabbage, the boys wanted only to go upstairs to sleep. But Grandfather Soar had noticed the pile of unseamed stockings on his daughter Ann's cot, as he had also noticed her red and swollen eyes.

"Looks like the womenfolk need a little help, boys," he said. "Grab a needle and let's show them how to seam stockings."

The three boys moaned loudly. But Ann brightened, and quickly brought her unfinished work to the table— dozens of flat-woven cotton stockings to be stitched up the back.

6

William jerked his head and opened his eyes. He had been dozing, a needle still in his hand and a stocking dangling from the thread. He looked around the table. Everyone was dozing, and the creamy white stockings were falling to the floor all around the table.

He glanced at his mother and thought it strange that she would fall asleep at any work. Then at the same moment he realized that she was praying—praying the same prayer over and over again.

"Please, God, there must be something more."

When she opened her eyes she looked directly across the table at William.

"It was so quiet in here, Mother," William whispered. "I think He heard, for sureness."

2

The American missionary said there was more and that Mary Taylor and her family were entitled to it. He said every man was entitled to happiness. He stood on the steps of the Beggarley Methodist Church and boldly preached that the ancient gospel of Jesus Christ had been restored to the earth—by angels.

Furthermore, he called all those who were honest in heart—those who loved virtue and hated vice—to flee to the Promised Land of America to build up the kingdom of God on earth. For, he said, the great and dreadful day of His Second Coming was nigh!

Then, lifting his voice above the clatter of the colliers, he sang with gusto:

> *Israel, Israel, God is calling,*
> *Calling thee from lands of woe;*
> *Babylon the great is falling.*
> *God shall all her towers o'er-throw.*
>
> *Come to Zion, come to Zion*
> *Ere his floods of anger flow.*
> *Come to Zion, come to Zion*
> *Ere his floods of anger flow.*

"Good tidings from Mount Zion," the missionary proclaimed at every door on Engine Lane.

But only Mary Taylor opened her door to Elder Bond from The Church of Jesus Christ of Latter-day Saints.

It was a Sunday evening in September. A gentle breeze wafted through the small kitchen window, carrying with it the strong smell of sulfur from the burning slag hills.

William sat with his family around the table, seaming stockings and listening to Elder Bond tell of the New Zion in the top of the Rocky Mountains of America.

In this high mountain valley, he said, each family lived in peace and prosperity, each man called the other "brother," and each man farmed his own land.

"No squires?" Grandfather Soar asked.

"No squires."

"And the Lord wants us to go there?" Mary asked.

"He wants you to gather to His kingdom," Elder Bond said. "It will not be easy, but I promise you it will be worth the sacrifice."

"We will go where He wants us," Mary said. "We are not accustomed to easy living. We are strong."

"But poor as a ragman's pocket," Grandfather Soar said. "How will we ever get to Zion?"

"By chartered ship across the Atlantic," Elder Bond explained. "By handcart across the interior. A new plan by our prophet, Brigham Young."

"Handcarts?" William asked.

"All provided with money loaned by the Church—not to be repaid until you have your own farm in the Valley. I will write a letter for you to the mission president in Liverpool."

"It's a dream belike," Mary said.

"It is true," the missionary said. Then leaning back in his chair, he sang of his faraway home:

O ye mountains high, where the clear blue sky
Arches over the vales of the free,
Where the pure breezes blow and the clear streamlets
    flow,
How I long to your bosom to flee!

O Zion! dear Zion!
Far o'er the sea,
My own mountain home, soon to thee will I come,
For my fond hopes are centered in thee.

As Elder Bond sang, William felt as if an angel from heaven were touching his soul. He would go where the Lord wanted him to go. And he would spend all his days building up His kingdom.

William looked around the small kitchen and out the window at the backyard, a small square of dirt with gray smoldering ash pits, owned forever by Thomas Barber, Esquire. He glanced at his pit clothes hanging up to dry near the fire, but never drying. And he knew Beggarley Bottom would not be hard to leave.

And if all his family believed—including Grandfather Soar, Ann, and Henry—it would not be hard at all. He looked back at the American missionary, singing of Zion, and his heart leaped for joy. He wanted to go to that place in the mountains.

3

There was a saying in England—"As poor as a stockinger." And from the appearance of Grandfather Taylor, William suspected it was true. Grandfather Taylor had holes in the seat of his trousers. All the Taylors had holes in their trousers because they sat all day long making stockings.

The Taylors lived in a two-room cottage in Hill Top, a mile east of Eastwood on the Nottingham Road. In the upstairs room were the quarters for the family—Grandfather Taylor with his sons and daughters and grandchildren. In the downstairs room were six framework knitting machines for making the knitted stockings. Big wooden frames filled the room, three on a side, leaving just a narrow aisle in the middle. The Taylors worked at the knitting machines all day long, and when darkness came they lighted paraffin tin lamps and worked late into the night.

Grandfather Taylor's family made the flat-woven stockings on their machines, and then Grandfather Soar's family, along with other families, seamed them up the back by hand. Every Saturday morning William or Jesse returned the seamed stockings to Grandfather Taylor and received the next week's supply; then Grandfather Taylor took a cartload of stockings to Nottingham. The boys took turns going with him.

Today it was William's turn. He wanted to frolic like a spring colt all the way to Hill Top because he wanted to tell Grandfather Taylor about America. But the two bags of stockings were so heavy and the ascent up Lynncroft so steep that William had to stop every few minutes to catch his breath.

Then too, he never liked to run very hard on the ground because there were men below, burrowing like moles through the earth, men flat on their backs hewing. How far down he did not know, but he knew they were there. They were his mates and had been for over three years.

He trod more carefully the last half mile to Hill Top, thinking how nice it was that there were no coal mines in America. How could there be, with all those heavy buffalo running around on top of the ground? No doubt the American Queen had made a law: "Because of our buffalo, no mines in America."

Without knocking, William poked his head in Grandfather Taylor's house. He never knocked because of the noise of the knitting machines.

"Hello," William shouted as he looked around the crowded room.

His two aunts looked up and nodded, but kept on with their work.

"Your grandfather's in the back, hitching up the cart," Aunt Eliza Leivers said loudly.

William nodded at her but did not smile. He never smiled at the aunts.

For years Grandfather Taylor had promised the next empty machine to William. But whenever there was a vacant seat, the aunts brought down another child from upstairs. William did not know how many more children

12

were upstairs waiting. He just knew he wanted to sit at a machine next to Grandfather Taylor—above the ground.

Had his father lived, things would have been different. His father, William Jesse Taylor, was Grandfather Taylor's oldest son—and his pride. As a young boy he had been apprenticed to a framesmith who taught him how to build the intricate machines. His father planned to build framework knitting machines and rent them to other stockingers. This would bring success to the Taylors!

It was a good plan. Grandfather Taylor told him this every time they journeyed to Nottingham. He could not seem to remember that his son had died of consumption ten years ago when William was just a baby.

William dropped his bags in the doorway and squeezed through the aisle to Uncle James's outstretched arms.

Uncle James, who was deaf, had never heard the hissing and the knocking and the clacking of the frames. Perhaps this was the reason, William thought, that Uncle James pressed his machine so hard through its courses and thumped his feet so hard on the treadles. Indeed, he was hard on knitting machines, and Grandfather Taylor was constantly shaking his head over the matter.

William moved back and watched his uncle work the knitting machine. His hands moved quickly—one hand throwing the thread over the row of needles, and the other passing the body of the frame through its motions. At the same time both feet were moving treadles at the base of the frame. And always his sharp eyes watched the thread and the needles and his hands and the treadles all at the same time.

Faster and faster Uncle James worked, and the machine hissed and knocked noisily. When the first inch of flat-knitted stockings appeared on his frame, he stopped, pointed to his miraculous work, and hugged William. And William hugged Uncle James.

How would he ever tell Uncle James about America?

The old horse was as rickety as the cart she pulled to Nottingham. And Grandfather Taylor was old and thin and raggedy. But William sat beside him at the front of the cart, proudly, holding the reins.

Nottingham was eight miles away, and it took half the day to journey there. But William was in no hurry. He had much to say to his grandfather today.

"Have you ever heard of America?" he asked.

Grandfather Taylor had heard of America. He said it was populated by savage red Indians who scalped every white man who stepped on their land.

"But Grandpa, I know a man from America, and he didn't get scalped."

"He was a lucky man."

Grandfather Taylor had heard about American missionaries. He said they came over to England to steal honest, hard-working people to be their slaves, and when the red Indians attacked, the slaves were sent out to fight them.

William shook his head. "No, Grandpa. It isn't that way. God wants us to gather to His kingdom on earth—in the top of the mountains in America."

"God wants you to do that?"

"You too, Grandpa. All of us."

Grandfather Taylor stroked his straggly gray whiskers. "And why in the top of the American mountains?"

"It's the Promised Land, Grandpa. A land of freedom."

14

"A land of savage red Indians," Grandfather Taylor concluded. "I would have chosen England." He took the reins because they had reached Nottingham.

The city was noisy and crowded, with many horse-drawn carts filling the narrow, littered streets. Dogs and people darted between the moving carts.

William thought it was exciting, but Grandfather Taylor sat stiffly, keeping one eye on the load of stockings until he reached a quiet back street that led to the warehouse.

Inside the crowded warehouse, men tossed bundles of stockings and yelled and squabbled like housewives on market day.

William and his grandfather joined the crowd and carried their bundles to a long wooden counter.

"Forty-eight dozen," Grandfather Taylor said proudly.

A young clerk hurriedly counted the stockings. Then he nodded to another man sitting on a high stool behind a cash box.

"Six pounds, two shillings, and fourpence," the cashier said, handing the money down to Grandfather Taylor.

Back in the cart Grandfather Taylor sat looking at the money in his hand, enjoying it for a few minutes. It was a great deal of money, he explained to William; however, after he paid the rent for six machines, paid for machine repairs, paid the charges for winding the yarn, paid the seamers, paid for the many, many needles, and paid for the paraffin candles, there would be scarcely a shilling left for bacon.

As they rode home, Grandfather Taylor explained again the plan of his oldest son, William Jesse, who had been resting in the parish churchyard for ten years.

William nodded, but because he knew it all from memory, he thought his own thoughts—about America. And as

15

the old horse dragged the cart into Hill Top, he asked, "Will you go with us—Jesse and me—if we go to America?"

Grandfather Taylor shook his head and pronounced, "Heresy and foolishness! Heresy and foolishness!"

William put his arm around his frail old grandfather, who was too old to journey to America. Almost too old to journey to Nottingham.

Grandfather Taylor knew many things, but he did not know very much about America. One thing for certain that he did not know was that if a person in America had holes in his trousers, he would simply toss them into the Mississippi River.

4

Before Jesse went down into Moorgreen Pit, he used to ask William why he always carried a stick, and William answered, "I tap on the walls to keep me company."

When Jesse turned eight and went into the pit, William gave him a stick. Then he told him the real reason. "Tap the walls as you crawl along, and if they crumble at all, back out fast!"

Uncle John and his mate could keep three putters busy hauling out the coal they cut. The two men lay on their backs and hacked with their picks at the coal above them, or they sat on their heels to strike against it. In the stifling hot stalls they threw of their heavy pit clothing and worked unencumbered like animals of the soil.

William and Jesse and Henry were their putters. Each boy wore a harness around his waist with a chain between his legs attached to a small wooden tram. On hands and knees the boys dragged the trams of coal through the low dark tunnels to the pit shaft, where the coal was raised to the surface.

It was the last day of September. The boys were hauling trams so fast that they had to wait on Uncle John and his mate.

"You're gettin' too fast for putters," Uncle John had said this morning. "Too fast."

Returning from the main shaft, William lagged behind Jesse and Henry. He pulled his empty tram absent-mindedly, dreaming of his cabbage farm in the Rocky Mountains of America.

It wouldn't be hard for him to recognize his farm there, in the green valley surrounded by high mountains, under the clear blue sky, with pure breezes blowing, and clear streamlets flowing, just as the missionary said.

Suddenly William bumped headfirst into a low wooden door.

"Eh there, Hank. Wake up!" he shouted. He rubbed his head, then tapped on the door with his stick. "Couldn't you hear me coming?"

There was a scuffling sound on the other side of the door, and a voice cried, "I wasn't asleep, just sittin'." As the little trapper pulled a ragged rope, the heavy, squeaking ventilation door opened.

William strained to see the boy at the door, but he could see nothing in the pitch-blackness.

"You're not Hank," he said. "What's your name?"

"I won't be tellin'. You will report to the Superior as how I was sleepin'."

"No, I won't. My name is William."

"Don't matter what your name. No one cares about a putter, not even God himself." The little trapper sneered and pulled the squeaking door shut.

William crawled on down the dark tunnel. He tried to recapture the image of his cabbage farm in the Rocky Mountains, but it had vanished. The dream itself seemed so unreal to William that he laughed aloud, and his laughter echoed down the tunnel.

How could God see him, William Taylor, down in the bottom of Moorgreen Pit?

18

Uncle John sat up on his heels in his stall. Black rivulets of water rolled down his face.

"I know you're too fast for a putter, William," he said proudly. "But—"

"No exceptions for me, Uncle John," William said.

"Tell you what," Uncle John said. "Samuel Clark is hewing alone this week—his mate laid up with pneumonia, breaking his body trying to keep up his stint." He sighed. "And I suppose, William, if it's to be the life of a collier, you might as well try hewing at the coal face. Samuel would welcome you."

William grinned. "I'd welcome it too, Uncle John."

So William began hewing. He lay on his back next to Samuel Clark, hacking at the black coal above him.

Samuel was glad for the help—and the company. He talked between strikes with his pick.

"Think we're—to London town—yet?" he asked.

"Don't know," William gasped.

"What would—you say—if you popped up—in front—of the Queen?"

"I'd say—I'd say—" William gasped for breath—"Well, now, I'd say—Your Majesty—"

"Aye—but then—what?"

"Don't know."

William tried hard to keep up with Samuel Clark, who worked at the same steady pace even while talking.

"Easy does it," Samuel said, chuckling. "You have—a lifetime—to hack away—down here."

"By the way," he added, "I don't think—we're headed—London way. Sounds—more like—we are under —the North Sea. But I hope not. I'm not afraid—of any- thing, mind you, but if there's anything—I don't take to— it's—"

19

William never knew what Samuel Clark was afraid of, because at that moment the roof of the stall dropped, and the two colliers were covered.

The next thing William knew, someone was pounding on his back, crying, "Breathe, Willy, breathe!" It sounded like Jesse far away.

William struggled for breath, choking and coughing.

"Samuel—" he sputtered.

"Don't talk!" It was Henry, lifting him by the arms, dragging him. "Uncle John has him."

Moorgreen Colliery closed that day at noon, its headstock wheels motionless against the sky, its shrill whistle screeching death.

Uncle John and his mate carried the body of Samuel Clark home to his wife. All his mates followed behind, black-faced and solemn.

Afterwards, the three putters fled behind the row houses and the ash pits to Beggarley Brook, where they sat among the willows, throwing rocks into the water and coughing.

"You were lucky, William," Henry said, smearing his face with his neck scarf.

"Aye," Jesse agreed.

"I been thinking," William said. "Mayhappen it wasn't just luck. I been thinking the Lord really wants me in His kingdom. And even if it's on the top of a very rocky mountain, I'm going!"

5

October and November passed with no letter from Liverpool. William's family had never received a letter before, but then, they had never sent one. There was a man who rode horseback from Nottingham just to deliver letters. William had seen him before, riding up to Lambclose House.

The mail carrier would no doubt think when he rode up to Engine Lane that no one there could pay the delivery charge for a letter. But he would be surprised. The Taylor family had saved coins from the stockings purposely.

In December when William was not thinking about the letter, he was thinking about the annual Christmas orange. He decided, however, that this year he would not go to Lambclose House to queue up for an orange.

Henry was not going. He was twelve, but big as fifteen, and he did not want to be the biggest boy in the long line for Barber's Annual Christmas Charity for Children.

Thomas Barber, Esquire, lived in Lambclose House high on a hill above Moorgreen Lake, secluded in a patch of dense woods. He rode around his vast estates on his fast Arabian mare and watched his turnips and cabbages growing, and he rode around to his six mines and peered down the shafts from high on his mount.

And every year, the day after Christmas, he gave out

oranges to the children of the poor. It was the butler who passed them out. Under his scrutinous eye the children were allowed to walk up the steep front steps of the brown stone mansion to look through the doorway at a gigantic glowing Christmas tree. At the bottom of the steps the butler handed out the oranges, one bright, fragrant orange to each child.

Each December William debated whether he should eat the orange immediately since he had waited so long for it, or carry it home and place it gleaming and fragrant in the middle of the table to enjoy a few days longer. Each December William and Henry and Jesse talked and talked about it and decided exactly what they would do. And then, usually, they did just the opposite.

But this Christmas Henry said he was too big. And if Henry did not go, how dare William?

Perhaps this year Squire Barber might change his mind. Instead of asking his butler to pass out the oranges, maybe he would ask his twelve-year-old son, who rode another fast Arabian mare around his father's estates looking for boys gathering mushrooms. And whenever he saw boys crawling through his woods, he lashed them with his long leather whip, and said if he ever saw them on his land again, he would wind the whip around their necks and drag them behind his horse.

After all, it was just an orange. And next Christmas William would be in America, where oranges rolled down the streets like pebbles, and the American women picked them up in their aprons to keep them from rolling into the ocean.

The day after Christmas was cold, and the line at Lambclose House was long. William, Jesse, and Henry stood at the end of the line, coatless, but with long woolen scarves tied around their necks and pulled up over their red noses.

They took turns leaving the line to check the activities at the front steps. There they saw the liverymen unloading the crates of oranges, and they saw the house servants scurrying up and down the steps, sweeping away puffs of snow.

Finally, after the liverymen had gone, the servants lined up and down the steps like marble statues. All was hushed. Then as the tall doors slowly opened, a figure stepped out clad in a long black cape, a black top hat, and a red neck scarf. Proud and arrogant, he descended the stairs with his head high—so high that William thought surely he would never see the last step.

It was the butler.

6

The letter lay on the table, open but unread. Though William had gone to dame school the winter he was five, he could not decipher all of the heavy black script. But he did not need to read it. A letter meant that a ship would be leaving Liverpool for America—and that there was room on that ship for him!

May 24, 1856, was a misty day, thinking of rain. In the hawthorne thicket by the Eastwood Railway Station, brown-speckled thrushes whistled their noisy songs. William sat in the second-class carriage across from his mother and Jesse. He had said good-bye, and now he sat looking out the open sides of the carriage at everyone he knew.

The Taylor family were standing tall and solemn with an air of melancholy about them. Never before had William seen all the Taylors standing at the same time. He realized for the first time that he looked like his father's family—slender in build with dark hair and dark brooding eyes. Perhaps he looked just like his father.

He smiled at the aunts, Aunt Eliza and Aunt Phoebe with all their children, and forgave them.

And Grandfather Taylor. He stood with one arm around Uncle James, who was weeping openly into his big hands. How could he leave Uncle James and Grandfather Taylor?

The Soars were all smiling, sad smiles. Uncle John stood above all the others holding his two little girls, waving. Little Aunt Elizabeth. Uncle Thomas and Aunt Sarah.

And together, holding on to each other, were Henry and Ann and Grandfather Soar—Grandfather Soar so conditioned to squires that he would not break his work bond even for America.

William swallowed hard. How could he be leaving Henry and Grandfather Soar? If this new religion was to make him so happy, why was he leaving them?

A gentle rain began falling. For a moment William wondered how big a puddle it would make at the bottom of Moorgreen Pit. He glanced at Jesse. His younger brother looked sick, leaning against their mother's arm, tears rolling down his cheeks. And William hardly recognized his mother sitting so stiff and pale.

Quickly he looked out of the carriage again. Everyone he knew was standing there holding on to each other with thin arms. And rising out of the mist behind them was the tall bell tower of the parish church where his father rested. Everyone he knew.

Although he did not want to leave them standing so helpless in the rain, he felt a strange sense of relief when the train jerked forward.

II
The Noise of Many Waters

1

Lime Street, Liverpool, was magnificent. Flanking the wide street were massive granite and marble buildings, glistening in the sunlight. From these halls, grand stairways led into open courts where ladies with parasols and gentlemen in silk top hats stolled among graceful statuary and brilliant flowers. And in the street's thoroughfare, elegant black coaches were drawn by high-stepping horses.

The Taylors from Eastwood stepped out of the Lime Street Railway Station with their bedrolls and canvas knapsack and looked about.

"Is this still England?" Jesse asked, wide-eyed.

"Where's the ship?" William asked.

Their mother took the letter from her pocket. "Sit you on our baggage, and I will inquire," she whispered. "Mind you, don't move. Remember the runners!"

William and Jesse nodded. Elder Bond had told them about boardinghouse runners—men who snatched luggage from emigrants and who led them to dishonest boardinghouses. Even those wearing official badges could not be trusted, he had said.

The boys sat on the bedrolls back to back, Jesse facing Lime Street and William facing the railway station.

Passengers from the station milled around them. Those

29

in simple cloaks and heavy boots, encumbered with bags and boxes like the Taylors, flocked west toward the harbor. Fashionably dressed passengers attended by porters blended readily into the Lime Street throng.

"Have you seen any runners yet?" Jesse whispered.

"No. Have you?"

"I'm not sure. Two or three people have looked at me. What do runners look like anyway?"

"Oh, they look different from other men," William said. "They look like runners. You'll be seeing one afore long."

Jesse eyed every passing face, but before he saw a runner, his mother returned. And he was glad.

The streets to the waterfront were narrow and dirty and crowded with people. Everyone seemed to be moving in one direction, carrying bedrolls and boxes and straw bundles and cabbages and babies. Street vendors cried their wares. "Trusses o' straw! Trusses o' straw! Cabbages!" On every door was a placard listing fast-sailing ships to New York and Boston.

"If all these people are going to America," William said, "there will be no room left for us." He pushed forward with such gusto that he bumped into Jesse and their mother, who had stopped to look up. And then William looked up.

Liverpool Harbor was a forest of trees! Hundreds of tall pine masts rose above hundreds of ships anchored in the vast stone piers of the harbor. And behind the tall ships, small black steamboats and dark red sailboats dotted the muddy waters of the river Mersey.

"Good lawks!" William exclaimed. "Hurry along!"

"Cabbages an' cheese! Tin pots an' pans!" peddlers shrieked.

"Slow down, Willy!" their mother called.

Holding on to each other and their baggage in a crooked

30

string, the family moved north along the wharf and gazed up at the magnificent ships, their wooden bowsprits like long necks stretching over the stone piers.

They stared at the strange figureheads high up under the bowsprits—carved wooden maidens with flaming red cheeks and black corkscrew curls, quizzical centaurs and mermaids, birds of prey, and spotted sea serpents posed to strike.

They wondered at the brave names painted on the ships, which William read choppily: "The *Ocean Queen*, the *Republic*, the *Lady Washington*, the *Columbia*, the *Freedom*, the *Champion*—and the *Horizon*."

"Here she is!" William exclaimed. "The *Horizon*!"

The *Horizon* lay anchored in Bramley Moore Dock. She was a big American packet ship—sixteen hundred tons, full-rigged with three masts reaching tall into the sky. From her bow a glassy-eyed eagle with a long orange beak spread its painted wings for flight. In her deep hold, the *Horizon* had carried a cargo of pig iron and timber across the ocean to Liverpool. Now she awaited her return load—emigrants to America.

The Taylors gazed up at the big ship.

"Well, boys," Mary said. "Well. And how do we get up on it?"

William picked up his mother's bedroll and slung it over his back. Someone had to take charge on this journey and, after all, he had been twelve since January.

"Follow me," he said, and he strode around the front of the ship to the gangway. Whistling, he marched up the wooden planks, with Jesse and Mary following.

William walked over to a seaman, who looked important in his white trousers and blue jacket, and showed him the letter.

"Can you tell me where our quarters are, sir?"

The first mate growled. "Main hatch."

"And where is that?"

"Follow yer nose!"

William beckoned to Jesse and his mother. "Main hatch," he called.

They looked down into the opened dark hatchway.

"Down here?" Mary Taylor asked. "I cannot see how to go down."

"Faith, turn your body 'round and climb down the ladder," a voice spoke pleasantly. Then a head emerged through the darkness.

"I'm Sister McBride," the woman said. "And 'tis right cozy we'll be after we get used to it. How old your boys be?"

"Ten and twelve," Mary answered.

"Sure and they go down with you," Sister McBride said. "If they were fourteen they would go to separate quarters. Single men at the bow, single women at the stern, and the families between. 'Tis a right good system, I'm thinkin'."

The steerage, William decided, as he stood at the bottom of the ladder waiting for his eyes to adjust to the darkness, was much like Moorgreen Pit: cold and damp and dark, with an occasional dull flicker from a horn lantern. Because the portholes were closed, the air was stifling. Hundreds of bewildered people were pushing and stumbling, carrying boxes and crying babies.

"Move on," someone shouted. "Find a bunk or move on!"

In the fitful light the Taylors could see the bunks along the two sides of the hold—three tiers of wooden boxlike spaces. They shoved their bedrolls into the first empty bunk and crawled in after.

When they sat up, they bumped their heads.

"Wait here," William said, "and I'll check out the others."

He climbed to the middle bunk, then the top bunk. He lay on his stomach and called down to his mother and Jesse.

"They are all made for tinety midgets," he said. "But," he whispered, "I think if the ship leaks we would be safest in the top bunk."

The family soon settled themselves in the top bunk. They discovered that the ceiling beams curved, allowing enough room for one person to sit up toward the aisle.

They watched other families finding bunks and settling down, as earlier others had watched them. The newcomers spread straw on the bunks and rolled out their quilts on top, then hung tin cups on nails in the bunk partitions and tied down pans and jugs with twine.

Mary looked at her boys. "I'm afraid we didn't read all of the letter," she whispered.

"It was too long," William said.

"If you boys will stay in the bunk," Mary said, "I will go over to one of the shops and buy some cups and straw."

"I'll go," William said.

"We will both go," Jesse added.

"Go to a shop then, together. And come right back," Mary said. "Take this shilling." She emptied the knapsack and handed it to William. "Buy three tin cups and a jug for water. And put them in here. And Jesse can carry a truss of straw."

"Don't worry about a thing," William said, crawling out of the bunk. "Come on, Jesse. Follow me."

The boys walked across the wharf and entered a crowded shop. Everything imaginable for a sea voyage was inside, piled on shelves and counters and hanging from the ceiling. It was a wonderful place to spend an afternoon, and the boys were tempted. But they made their purchases quickly as they had promised and started back to the ship.

Two runners were waiting outside, one on each side of the doorway. One man tripped Jesse with his foot, grabbed the truss of straw, and ran. As William reached over to help Jesse, the other man grabbed the knapsack.

"Eh, stop!" William clung to the knapsack and kicked at the man.

The burley thief cursed and hit William, sending him sprawling. He grabbed the knapsack and turned to run, but Jesse held him by his shirt. The man whirled around and knocked Jesse down. The back of his green shirt went down with Jesse.

"Two wild ones," the man muttered.

William sat up, dazed, just in time to see the man run down the wharf with the knapsack. He struggled to his feet and ran after the man, crying, "Stop, thief, stop!"

The runner turned up a side street and William followed. As he pushed through the crowded street, he could occasionally catch a glimpse of the man's ragged green shirt. But at the end of the block he could no longer see the man, and the street he was on forked out into three streets. He paused, then continued straight ahead, running blindly. After a while he began turning into streets on the right, hoping somehow to find the thief.

Suddenly he was grabbed by two men. One held his arms and stood on his boots while the other went through his pockets.

"He's too big for a sweep," the first man said, scowling.

"Lucky for him." The other man laughed.

The thieves found the change from the shilling in his pocket, spat in his face, and disappeared.

William slumped against a wall to catch his breath and wipe his face. Slowly he began to comprehend his situation. He was undoubtedly lost. He had lost his mother's knapsack and her shilling. But worse than that—a hot wave of guilt swept over him—he had lost Jesse. And Jesse was just the right size for a chimney sweep!

William cried out in agony, "Jesse! Jesse!"

He had to find Jesse. First he tried to retrace his steps, then he tried to remember the streets. But one street looked just like another. He ran desperately, turning right, turning left, trying to find any street that turned into the harbor.

As he ran, William stumbled over a broken cellar door and fell on his knees. He cried out from the stinging pain, and for a few minutes he sat hugging his knees. Soon he became aware of another cry, and he looked around, startled. Then he heard more cries, like those of little kittens. Peering cautiously into a dark cellar, he saw the pallid faces of crying children.

Horrified, he jumped up and ran. He ran past aged women curled up in doorways and crippled men begging. He ran past barefoot, ragged children. And he ran and ran and ran. When he felt certain that the ship had left without him and that he would spend the rest of his life running in these horrible streets, he ran headlong into a big policeman with a truncheon tucked under his arm.

The policeman looked down at William. "What are you doing on Tithebarn Street?" he asked.

William shook his head, too breathless to speak.

The policeman walked him to the end of the block, turned him facing west, and pointed with his truncheon.

"The harbor is straight in front of you, laddie," he said.

William's head throbbed as he ran down the long wharf, and he could feel blood trickling down his face. His left eye was swollen shut. But nothing mattered, nothing mattered at all—if Jesse would just be back at the ship.

On the gangway of the *Horizon*, William's mother and Jesse were waiting, and everything was right once again.

Down in the hold in their top bunk, Mary counseled her boys. "Trust in the Lord with all your hearts, boys. He will direct your paths. And mayhappen you won't get lost again!"

"And also," William added, "no one get off the ship afore it reaches America."

2

At five o'clock the next morning a bugle blared down the main hatch, and a voice roared, "All men on deck!"

William sat straight up in bed and knocked his head against the beams. He already had a lump on his head, and one eye was swollen shut. He moaned and slid back down in his quilt.

"Come on, get up," Jesse urged, tugging at him. "Eh, you do look terrible," he said. "But we have to go up on deck while the womenfolk dress. It's a rule."

Overnight the eight hundred emigrants had organized into wards, with Elder Edward Martin, a missionary returning home to the Great Salt Lake Valley, appointed president.

Upstairs, the first blast of the bugle brought the ship's captain out on the poop deck in his topcoat and bare feet. The first and second mates ran out from their cabins, and the crew tumbled out of the forecastle, wearing only their blue dungaree trousers, mumbling and cursing. The few bewildered cabin passengers stuck their heads out of their doors.

They all stared in disbelief as several hundred men from steerage ascended two hatchways, singing mightily. The men stood, singing, until the women and children joined them. Then all eight hundred knelt on the wooden deck planks to pray.

Elder Martin stood on a wooden crate near the foremast and addressed his assembled group.

"Modern Israel"—his voice thundered the length of the ship—"you have responded to the call of the Lord. You have left the iniquities of Babylon, and you are gathering— one of a city and two of a family—to Zion, the new Jerusalem, to build up the kingdom of God on earth."

The crowd cheered, and Elder Martin lifted his arms.

"You are fulfilling the words of the prophet Isaiah. You are gathering to the top of the mountains, where in these last days the Lord's house has been established."

Again the crowd broke forth with cheers, as the American missionary concluded. "My brothers and sisters, have peace among you and be of good cheer, for the Lord is pleased. And now let us sing of Zion."

"Sing," William whispered to Jesse, "and you won't hear your stomach growling."

Jesse grinned, and both boys sang so loudly their mother glanced sidelong in amazement.

> *Israel, Israel, God is calling,*
> *Calling thee from lands of woe . . .*

All morning the harbor was enveloped in mist and fog. William and Jesse walked the starboard side of the main deck, exploring. They met two other brothers who were doing the same thing—Thomas and James Briggs, weavers from Stalybridge, Lancashire. Even with their thick curly hair, they had a look of the Hill Top Taylors about them, as if they had sat long hours at their weaving looms.

"Look you!" Thomas Briggs pointed through the mist. "Tugboats."

The boys strained to see the tugboats, which were puffing and tooting, waiting to be fastened to the *Horizon* as soon as her hawsers were cast off.

"And look—the captain has come out!" Jesse exclaimed.

The boys looked to the after end of the ship and saw the captain on the poop deck, greeting an important-looking pilot who had just come aboard.

"Cast away!" the captain shouted.

Leaning over the railing, the boys watched while longshoremen on the dock unfastened heavy ropes, which hit and splashed in the brown, oily water. The sailors hauled them aboard.

Then the small steamboats, whistling and tugging, pulled the *Horizon* down the brown waters of the river Mersey on her way to the Irish Channel—and America.

As the ship moved from the harbor, the steerage passengers crowded on the deck. They gripped the ship's railing as the unfamiliar floor beneath them began to rock. They stood in drizzling rain, clutching their cloaks about them, as they strained for one last glimpse of their homeland before it gradually disappeared into the mist.

"I have an idea," Jesse said. "Let's walk the complete length of this ship, from the front to the back."

"From the bow to the stern," Thomas said. He had been listening to the crew talk.

"Let's do both," his brother James said.

They started at the bow, walking like clowns on the strange rocking floor.

"Something is wrong with me," Jesse shouted. "I can't walk straight."

"It's the floor," William said. "It slopes out from the center."

"And it's wet!" James cried, falling down.

The other boys, laughing, tumbled on top of James. They crawled to a companionway leading to the upper deck and climbed the steps.

The forecastle looked like a wharfside ship. It was crowded with wooden casks of water, salt horse barrels of meat, and ropes coiled into giant nests. From small pens, pigs squealed and chickens cackled.

"Look you at the ship's bell," James cried, hurrying over to examine the large golden bell.

"Git!" a sailor shouted.

"I wonder what's in here," Thomas said, pointing to a V-shaped cabin at the front of the ship.

The boys peered inside. The small cabin was lined with bunks; black sea chests and duffel bags were on the floor.

"It's the sailors' cabin," William said.

"See the straw mattresses?" Thomas whispered. "I saw a sailor carrying one on his back. He called it his donkey's breakfast."

"Out of here," a voice growled, and the boys jumped back. They peered into another small cabin, which they concluded was the water closet. They also agreed that it was much too dangerous for use, because they could see the rolling water beneath.

William was the first to spot the open hatch, portside on the main deck. "Let's go down there," he suggested.

"Mayhappen we shouldn't," Jesse said. "Mayhappen it's the quarters for the crew."

"We just saw their cabin," William said. "I think this is the lodging for the single men. Let's find out."

The boys climbed down into the darkness, and as their eyes adjusted, they saw that the room was filled with barrels and chests.

"It's a storage room," Thomas whispered.

As they turned to climb back up, the hatchway darkened. Someone was coming.

For a moment the boys stood terrified. Then they ducked behind a large wooden chest, hoping to dart up the ladder as soon as the danger passed.

Several seamen climbed down the ladder, carrying long poles, chisels, saws, and hammers. The last sailor, with a lantern, dropped the hatch cover behind him. Escape was impossible.

The sailors pounded on barrels and chests, looking for stowaways. They stopped a few yards from the frightened boys.

"How many ya wager we'll find this trip?" one sailor asked hoarsely.

"Don't matter how many," another said. "They'll be sorry!"

The men guffawed loudly.

The boys shrank as low as possible. They were trapped.

"Let's search a little, just to satisfy the mate," one of the sailors said. "And then we'll leave our tools behind this here barrel."

The others agreed. They hammered on top of several more barrels and turned a few upside down. They pried lids off chests and probed through them with a long pole with a nail on the end.

"Looks like the bloody tar will be wasted this trip," one said, tossing his hammer to the floor. "Anyway, there's no need lookin' longer. They'll all be at the bottom of the pond in the morning. All nine hundred and their bugle with 'em."

"Don't talk too plain," an old sailor growled. "Have ya loosened the boats?"

41

"Aye."

"In that corner then—midnight. And if the mate drops in, we'll start pounding on the barrels. We're thorough, we are."

"Aye, aye!"

"And in the morning we'll be back in Liverpool, and the Mormon rats will be at the bottom of the brine."

William was breathing so hard, he was afraid the sailors would hear him. He clutched Jesse's arm and glanced over at Thomas and James. They looked like ghosts.

The boys crouched behind the chest for what seemed forever—fearful that the sailors would find them, yet afraid they would leave and lock the hatch cover, trapping them below.

At last the sailors hid their tools. Then singing a loud, bawdy shanty, they climbed up the ladder, leaving the hatch cover open.

On deck, the four boys huddled together near the main mast and, watching out for the crew, whispered among themselves.

"Are we Mormon rats?"

"We are Mormons."

"What's a-matter with Mormons?"

"I don't know. But something must be."

"It's our bugle."

"We will have to tell the captain."

"He won't believe us."

"He won't even speak to us."

"We will have to tell Elder Martin."

Elder Martin was a tall, strong man with thick, wavy hair and a short beard. He looked at the four boys with steadfast eyes.

"Are you lads speaking the truth?"

42

They nodded and answered, "Yes, sir."

"Do you have the courage to face the captain of this ship?"

The boys looked at each other. Then they nodded slowly.

"Not for sureness, though," Jesse added.

Elder Martin laughed. "The Lord is on our side. Let's go."

The boys waited uneasily before the closed cabin door, now and then hearing the voices of Captain Reed and Elder Martin. Jesse twisted his cap until William took it and pulled it back into shape.

"Don't worry," William whispered. He put Jesse's cap back on his head.

Soon the door opened, and Captain Reed scowled at the boys.

"So these are the boys who can't mind their own business," he said. He puffed at his pipe.

The boys looked down at their boots.

"We were just looking about," Thomas said.

"And we overheard," William added.

The captain surveyed the boys, and his gaze finally stopped with William. He scrutinized the swollen black eye and the bruised forehead. He stared so long that William turned scarlet.

"So you're the troublemaker?" the captain asked, sneering.

"No," William said. He began explaining about the runners and the ceiling beams, but Captain Reed did not listen. He turned to Elder Martin.

"I'll test their word," he said, "but only because you ask it. They look like street ruffians to me."

"They are honest boys," Elder Martin said calmly.

43

"They are Mormon boys." He extended his hand to Captain Reed, who shook it somewhat reluctantly.

"You are a strange people, you Mormons," he said, shaking his head. "And I want no more trouble. And not a word of this to anyone. Understand?"

Elder Martin shook the captain's hand vigorously. "There will be no trouble from us, Captain."

The *Horizon* was towed out of the river Mersey into the Irish Channel, where the tugboats were dropped. The pilot returned with the tugs back up the river.

Now the first mate shouted at the crew to set the sails, and the sailors scurried up the ratlines into the high rigging. And when the mate gave the command, "Let go sail," the magnificent white sails were unfurled against the sky.

The secret the boys shared weighed heavily upon them, and they found no pleasure in watching the activities of the crew. They went down into the hold.

"I can't breathe," Jesse gasped as he stepped from the ladder.

"Hold your nose," William said. "Somebody's been sick on the floor!"

As the boys worked their way to their bunks, they realized almost everybody had been sick on the floor.

"Don't move me, boys. Don't even touch me," Mary whispered as the boys climbed up the bunks.

"What's a-matter, Mother?" Jesse asked.

"Sure and she be seasick like the rest of us," a voice wailed from an adjoining bunk. It was Sister McBride.

In two bunks nearby, members of the Briggs family were groaning and crying. Brother Briggs was holding two little girls, and Sister Briggs was holding two babies.

44

"Where have you boys been?" Sister Briggs scolded. "Hold these babies a minute. And why couldn't our Eliza stay in the same place as the rest of the family? I cannot manage be-out her. Here, dump these slop buckets for me."

She handed the two babies to Thomas and James. Then, as Jesse and William walked past, she handed the two buckets to them.

Thomas and James glanced hopelessly at their friends.

"She gets her children mixed up betimes," James said, embarrassed.

"That's all right," William said. "Come on, Jesse."

William and Jesse walked toward the hatchway, holding the buckets in front of them, trying not to breathe. But before they reached the hatchway, the ship rocked suddenly. And all the passengers in the *Horizon's* steerage were seasick, including the slop carriers.

William sat wrapped in a quilt at the bottom of the hatchway with Jesse leaning against him in a fitful sleep. He could hear the water splashing against the side of the ship, and he was filled with terror. He did not want the sailors to carry out their murderous plan, but neither did he want the captain to call him a liar. And if he did, what would the punishment be?

He imagined being dropped overboard for the sharks, or being sent back in a rowboat to Liverpool, never having enough money to get back to Grandfather Soar—just wandering in the harbor streets the rest of his life.

The ship's bell struck the hour. Was it eleven o'clock or twelve? William jumped up and climbed the ladder to check with Elder Martin, who was taking watch at the main hatch.

"It's only eleven o'clock, son," the missionary said. "Go back to sleep."

William crept back down the ladder and crawled into the quilt next to Jesse.

Jesse jumped up. "Is it time?"

"It's only eleven o'clock," William whispered. "Go back to sleep."

But neither William nor Jesse could sleep. After a while the Briggs boys joined them, and they all sat straining to hear any sounds on deck.

The ship rolled, and James cried. "They did it! We are sinking!"

"Hush!" his brother said.

Shortly before twelve o'clock there was a commotion on deck, and the boys climbed cautiously up the ladder.

"Elder Martin," William whispered.

There was no answer.

William climbed quickly out of the hatch. He saw Elder Martin, Captain Reed, and the crew gathered around the lifeboats. The sailors were silently lowering the boats over the side of the ship—at the point of Captain Reed's pistol.

At five o'clock the next morning the bugle sounded for morning prayers.

The new crew, just arriving by steam tug, assumed it was a welcome fanfare, and they cheered as they carried their sea chests and duffel bags to the forecastle.

Only a few steerage men responded to the bugle call. Most of the passengers were too sick to come up on deck for any reason. There were four passengers on the main deck, however, who were singing their hearts out, wrapped in quilts inside a gigantic circle of hawser rope. They were sorry everyone was sick. But they were also glad.

If everyone stayed sick for a few days longer, the new crew would not know there were 856 Mormons aboard until they were all out in the middle of the Atlantic Ocean.

3

The *Horizon* plowed her way through the choppy waters and drizzling rain of the Irish Channel, around Cape Clear on the western tip of Ireland, and out into the Atlantic Ocean toward her 3,000-mile-distant destination—Boston, Massachusetts, America. Out in the Atlantic her white sails billowed, and the wind hummed in her high rigging as she sped along under a cloudless blue sky.

"Flying-fish weather," the old sailmaker told William.

The sailmaker was the ship's carpenter. He set up his daily work of splicing ropes and patching sails on the main deck near the water barrels, where he could talk to the men waiting in line for water. He was old and bent. But he wore golden earrings to preserve his good eyesight—and he carried salt in his pockets for good luck.

William stood daily in the water line, and the old carpenter often spoke to him. And each day as soon as William finished taking the water jug down to his mother, he met Jesse and the Briggs boys at the rope pile behind the foremast for breakfast.

This warm May day he joined the other boys. Thomas and James each had a sister to tend, tied to the end of a short rope.

They ate their breakfast—stamping with their boots on

the hard sea biscuits to break them into pieces small enough to dunk into their tin cups.

"It's flying-fish weather," William announced.

"How do you know?" James asked.

"Look for yourself," William said calmly, and he lay on his back looking up into the white billowing sails.

The other boys plopped down on their backs and gazed up. They saw only the billowing sails and several seamen bobbing about high up in the rigging with their tar buckets.

"That's hard work," Thomas said.

"We have some hard work ahead of us," William said, "moving all those rocks in the Rocky Mountains."

"Why will we move them?" Jesse asked.

"I hear tell," William said, "as how we'll need rock walls twenty feet high around our farms to keep out the buffalo."

"Buffalo!" Thomas tugged gently at his rope to see if his little sister was still at the other end. "Mayhappen those buffalo will be our biggest problem then?" he asked.

"That's for sureness," William said decisively.

The two little Briggs girls clapped and squealed as they watched colorful fish leaping and gliding up above the railing of the ship. But the four boys dreaming of cabbage farms in the Rocky Mountains missed the flying fish.

One morning the old sailmaker said, "Storm's a'comin'. A whopper."

William looked skeptically at the old wrinkled man. He had just told William that if the sun beat down any hotter on deck, the tar between the planks would melt.

"How do you know?" William asked.

"My former colleagues are warnin' me," the sailmaker

said. He hobbled over to the railing and pointed down at the sea gulls bobbing about on the small waves.

"The gulls?"

"Look how they are washin' themselves—over and over again."

William stared.

"And do you see how dark the water is?" The old sailor continued. "The darker the water, the harder the storm. We're in for a whopper, laddie. A real whopper!"

The old man pulled from his pocket a small dark bottle of hartshorn. This lotion, he said, had been laboriously extracted from the antlers of a deer and was highly recommended for his "rumattic bones." He sat down on a crate and rubbed his legs.

Behind the foremast William casually remarked, "Storm's a-comin'."

Jesse, Thomas, and James stared at him.

"How do you know?" Jesse asked.

"Many ways," William said, dunking a sea biscuit into his tea. "One is that big sea gull over portside as keeps crying, 'Storm's a-comin', Willy. Storm's a-comin'.' "

The other boys jeered and rolled over each other. Then they lay on their backs looking up through the limp and graceless sails at the blue sky—waiting for the storm.

The old carpenter was right. The storm was a whopper. When it was only a dark spot no larger than a kite on the western water, Captain Reed strode across the poop deck and roared for the first mate who covered the length of the main deck on a dead run.

"Aye, aye, sir!"

Then the first mate cupped his hands around his mouth and breathlessly shouted the captain's orders. "Clear the decks! All hands on deck! All hands on deck!"

The call brought immediate action. High up in the rigging the seamen instantly unhooked their pots of tar and began climbing and sliding down to the deck. Seamen tumbled out of their cabin in the forecastle, half asleep, scowling at the first mate.

The second mate dispersed the water line and began lashing the water barrels to the side of the ship.

"All passengers below," he hollered.

The decks were crowded with sailors and passengers rushing to obey the officers' commands.

And as soon as the sailors who had been up in the sails reached the deck, the first mate bellowed another order.

"Aloft, men. Reef those sails!"

The old carpenter gathered up his tools and materials and started for his cabin. The four boys ran to help him.

"Didn't you lads hear the second mate?" he asked.

"We want to help," Jesse said.

"I could use some younger legs," the old sailor said, smiling. He handed part of his load to the boys.

The boys were hurrying back from the carpenter's cabin, almost in reach of the main hatch, when the storm hit. Suddenly the bow of the *Horizon* was lifted up out of the water as if by a giant chain. The frenzied sea rose higher and higher, then crashed down on the ship.

The four boys sprawled face down on the wooden deck and rolled helplessly toward the after end of the ship. William bumped against the ship's bulwark, but could find nothing to grasp.

"Jesse," he shouted. "Hold on!"

The wind shrieked through the ship, ripping sails into ribbons and blowing them out to sea. Dark green waves swirled over the railing, covering William so he could see nothing.

51

"Jesse," he gasped. "Jesse!"

William heard only the roar of the waves and the creaking of the old wooden hull as the ship strained to right herself. Then as he struggled to a crawling position, he felt the deck tilt in the opposite direction, and the *Horizon* plunged into the roaring sea. He was swept back down the deck, but as he passed the main mast he grabbed a rope and held on with all his strength.

Suddenly he became aware of Brother Briggs, his two boys, and Jesse, drenched with water, holding up the cover to the main hatch. The second mate crouched over them, ferociously swinging a hammer.

"Git that door down before I knock it down," he yelled. "That rascal deserves to drown!"

Before the ship plunged again, William inched his way over to the hatchway, where he was pulled to safety. His mother stood on the ladder, wet and shivering and very pale.

"Sorry, Mother," he gasped. "I didn't mean to worry you."

"It's all right now, Willy. But you have no sea blood in you. Remember that."

The hatch cover banged shut. With the hatch and the portholes closed, the hold was in total darkness. William reached for his mother and Jesse, and they waded through ankle-deep water to their bunk.

Then, over the rattling of tin cans and the crying of children, William heard a sound that struck absolute terror into his soul. The second mate was nailing down the hatch cover.

In the dark hold of the ship, the passengers waited

helplessly in their bunks. In the deep darkness they had somehow managed to collect their children and their belongings and tie them to their bunks. Some had been lucky enough to receive their daily water supply before the second mate ordered them below, but most had returned to their bunks with empty jugs.

Nearly all were seasick, and what few buckets for refuse could be found in the dark were insufficient. The salty bilge water on the floor soon became a splashing sewer.

The storm raged on. It was impossible to know day from night. Occasionally someone would climb the ladder and beat against the hatch cover, demanding that it be unlocked. But no one unlocked the cover. Perhaps, William thought, there were no sailors or captain or missionaries left to unlock the hatch.

As the ship lurched and rocked, Mary tried to comfort her boys. "Do not be afraid, boys. The Lord is with us. And the Lord is mightier than all this water."

"Then why are we so miserable?" Jesse cried.

"Good-dear-a-me," she said. "I do not know. But I do know as how the Lord chastens those he loves. And mind you," she said, "it matters not when the end comes. It matters only with what courage we reach the end."

William woke with a pounding headache, gasping for air. He tried to move but found that Jesse had rolled on top of him. He squirmed free of Jesse and turned facing the hull of the ship.

The pounding continued, and he suddenly realized that it was against the side of the ship, just above his head.

A shark! A shark striking at the hull of the ship! And in a few minutes the sharp jaws would come through the wooden planks. And then the sea—

William held his hands against the ship's side, against the banging of the shark. He wanted to scream, but his voice made only a dry, hollow sound. He reached to waken his mother but discovered she was already awake kneeling on the bunk, praying.

Jesse grabbed his arm. "Do you hear that noise, Willy?"

"Aye."

"What do you think it is?"

William's voice was raspy. "Some old log adrift. Don't worry."

"Mayhappen that old sea gull as you were telling us about?"

"For sureness." William swallowed hard.

"Do you think it is going to break through?"

"No. Never a chance."

Jesse was silent for a minute. Then in a trembling voice he whispered, "Are you afraid, Willy?"

"No. Now put your arms over your ears."

William turned on his stomach and pressed his face into the ragged quilt. In the darkness he cringed with fear and shame. Now that the end had surely come, he had not endured. He would meet his Maker after telling four falsehoods in a row.

The storm lasted for three days and nights. On the third night the *Horizon* took a deep plunge and then, with a tremendous shudder as if ridding herself of the annoyance of the storm, she righted herself on an even keel. The storm was over.

4

As the days passed, the steerage passengers became accustomed to the constant rolling of the ship. They sought the sunwashed decks eagerly, sitting in groups, washing and mending clothes. They had been on the water for three weeks. It was June now. The women talked of home, of the blossoming hawthorne and myrtle.

The drinking water from the wooden barrels had all been used, and now the iron barrels were brought up on deck. The water was red with rust.

"Add vinegar," the second mate suggested.

The lines to the cooking galley seemed longer and slower. The potatoes issued were soggy and sour, the salt pork rancid.

In the deep hold the bilge water splashed ankle-deep. Many passengers left their bunks to sleep on the open deck. Many others, however, were so ill that they had never been on deck since the ship left Liverpool. The organization of a new committee, in addition to the ones Elder Martin had organized at Liverpool, became necessary—a louse committee.

Each morning those steerage passengers who were able rallied forth at the five o'clock reveille and thanked God that they were on their way to Zion. And at night they sang songs of praise and offered fervent prayers of thanksgiving that they were one day closer to their destination.

On moonlit nights they assembled in groups on the main and quarter decks, singing and dancing to Brother McBride's fiddling.

"Look you at our mother," Jesse said one night to William.

The boys watched their mother, who was dancing a polka with a whiskered gentleman.

"When did she learn to do that?" William asked.

Jesse shook his head. "Afore we were born, for sureness."

"She's smiling," William commented. "I guess she doesn't mind it."

They watched their mother dance until Thomas and James tugged at their arms.

"There's a game over ahind the main mast," James said. "Let's go."

A group of young people were playing "Drop the Handkerchief," and, as the four boys approached, the circle of arms opened to include them.

Sailors idled away their time watching the game, cheering and betting. They lounged against the mast and the water barrels, chewing quids of tobacco. The old carpenter sat on a crate playing a doleful tune on a comb. He stopped each time the handkerchief was dropped.

The girls had the handkerchief, and it looked as if they intended to keep it. Time after time a girl ran around the circle and dropped the handkerchief to another girl. Then they both raced for the empty space, squealing like little pigs. Then the game began over again with a girl chanting:

> *"I have a little doggy and he won't bite you,*
> *And he won't bite you and he won't bite you."*

Not interested in squealing girls, William looked through the circle at the sailors spitting their tobacco juice straight over the railing out to sea. One sailor, chewing vigorously, seemed to be shooting at a target. A sea gull perhaps, William thought, or even better, one of those flying fish.

The monotonous chant continued:

> *"And he won't bite you, and he won't bite you,*
> *And he won't bite you, but he will bite you!"*

William was still watching the sailor when Jesse poked him. "Go, Willy!" he cried.

By the time William picked up the handkerchief and started running, the squealing girl was halfway around the circle. In the next instant she was in his place, laughing and clapping her hands.

The sailors roared with laughter and stomped their feet on the deck. The young people snickered. William stood bewildered, looking at the skinny girl in a brown dress who had beaten him. The girl laughed jubilantly, her dark eyes flashing and her black hair falling against her face.

The commotion attracted the attention of several adults who, upon checking their pocket watches, clucked over the lateness of the hour. Quickly they hurried to the main mast and scurried the young people down to bed.

The Taylor family lay in their top bunk too excited for sleep. They whispered in the darkness.

"We saw you dancing, Mother," Jesse said softly. "We didn't know you knew it."

"You did it main good," William said.

57

"Thank you, boys," she whispered. "Your father and I danced betimes." She sighed. "I saw your game, too."

"Did you see the girl as tricked me?" William asked hesitantly.

"Yes, William. She did that because she knows who you are. I have become acquainted with her mother, Sister Stones. And her father grew up in Eastwood. He's a collier."

"What's her name?"

"Hannah Rachel. She's the oldest of the four children. Ten years old, I believe Sister Stones said."

Hannah Rachel. Hannah Rachel. William pulled the quilt up to his chin and rolled over on his side facing the hull. Hannah Rachel would not outsmart him again!

5

When William threw a bucket of refuse over the railing the next morning, he noticed that the refuse from the previous night was still with the ship. The ship was not moving!

William looked up at the sails and saw that they were limp and sagging. He looked over the railing again. The ocean was a blue mirror, reflecting back his image. There was not a wave nor a ripple in sight. The *Horizon* had stopped in the middle of the Atlantic Ocean.

The old sailmaker said that a calm was a curse upon the ship and that she might float lifeless like this for days or months—and nothing the captain or crew could do would move her. He nodded toward the poop deck high above the after end of the ship. William, looking up, could see Captain Reed pacing back and forth, his hands gripped behind his back.

"Sometimes," the carpenter whispered, "the skipper walks right over the side into the sea."

William and his friends gathered around the sailmaker. "Why is there a curse on the ship?" William asked.

"Can't say for certain," the old sailor said, shaking his head. "Could be as we set sail on a Friday."

"But we left Liverpool on a Sunday," Jesse said.

"It's the preachers then. Sea gods get angry."

"The missionaries? Elder Martin and Elder Haven and Elder Waugh?" The boys were astounded.

"Last time I sailed with a preacher," the old man said, putting down his tools, "I was on a clipper bound for Australia. Storms lashed at her all down the Atlantic and around South Africa, until her canvas hung in ribbons.

"Then"—the carpenter shook his head—"in the middle of the Indian Ocean she lay becalmed for three weeks. Three weeks under the scorching sun. Not a breeze. Not a wave. Motionless on a sea of glass. Cursed by the sea gods."

"What happened?" the boys asked.

The old sailor squinted until his eyes were two thin lines.

"The preacher was thrown overboard," he said, "like Jonah of old. And the next morning a sou'wester came up—and the ship sailed again."

The four boys looked at the wizened old man skeptically.

"Just because he was a preacher?" Jesse ventured.

"That's reason enough, laddie."

The boys questioned no further. They knew about the carpenter's golden earrings and the salt in his pockets. And they also remembered the first crew at Liverpool.

"Sailors are superstitious," Jesse said later in the day as the boys were walking the port side of the *Horizon*, scanning the sullen waters.

The others agreed, but they did not race about the deck as usual nor join the other young people in the games.

On the third day of the calm the boys met for breakfast, as usual, behind the foremast. They watched the sailors slinking about the teakwood decks, jumping at their own shadows.

"Do you see how the crew keeps looking with crooked eyes at the missionaries?" Thomas asked.

The other three boys nodded.

"Sailors are superstitious," Jesse said again.

"Well, their old sea gods won't save them," James said, scoffing. He stomped hard on a sea biscuit, smashing it.

"Doesn't look like ours is going to save us, either," Thomas said quietly.

Jesse twisted his cap in his hands.

"Listen," he said. "Everyone is praying every morning and every night. The missionaries are praying for their converts, and the converts are praying for the crew. And the crew—they're praying to their old sea gods to save the ship!"

Jesse paused, then went on. "So who is praying for the missionaries? They are the ones as are in trouble!"

William, Thomas, and James nodded agreement.

Then William pulled off his cap. *"We* will," he said solemnly.

On the fourth morning of the calm, William tossed a bucket of refuse over the side of the ship, and he saw that the ship was beginning to move.

The sailors also saw, and they began adjusting ropes and climbing up the rigging, cheering and singing a ragged shanty. Captain Reed, standing on the poop deck, smiled in satisfaction.

William looked for the old sailmaker, but he was not in his usual place on deck. He ran to the carpenter's cabin near the forward end of the ship and knocked hard on the door.

"We are moving," he shouted. "We're moving! We are out of the calm!"

The carpenter came quickly to the door, brushing his hands through his thin gray hair.

"We're moving!" William repeated, breathlessly. "We are out of the calm!"

The sailmaker smiled broadly and clasped William's hands. He shook his old gray head in disbelief, and his earrings sparkled in the sunlight. Then he looked steadily into William's eyes. "Somebody must of tempted fate," he said, "and whistled in the wheelhouse."

William grinned. "Or something like that," he said. "Something like that."

6

Lifted from the calm, the *Horizon* sped before a steady wind, like a great sea bird, toward the shores of America.

On the last day of June—just over five weeks from Liverpool—land was sighted. The travelers swarmed on deck, each trying to be the first to see America. They were weakened, thin, and sick. But what did it matter? The long ocean voyage was over.

They scrubbed their bunks with all the strength they had left and threw their rags and straw overboard. They wanted to be worthy and clean to enter the Promised Land.

When they saw over the ship's bow the gray shores of Cape Cod, they shouted, "Hosanna, hosanna!" And as the ship was towed into Constitution Wharf in Boston Harbor, they knelt on the wooden decks and thanked God.

William wanted to be the first one to step foot on America—but how did everyone get in front of him? Though he could hear music and laughter, he could see nothing except the backs of people and their boxes. He tossed his bedroll over his shoulder and turned to his mother and Jesse.

"Follow me," he said, too impatient to wait longer, and he pressed forward through the passengers and boxes to the gangway.

As William saw America, his heart leaped for joy. For a

moment he stood gripping the railing at the top of the gangway and stared, unable to believe what he saw.

On the wharf a band was playing, and on both sides of the gangway American ladies were tossing oranges to the surprised, laughing children.

William gripped the railing harder, unable to move. The crowd behind him pushed and poked, but he held his place, looking in wonderment.

There were no squires, no butlers. Just men from a tract society blasting "Yankee Doodle" from their horns, and women in gray dresses and bonnets handing out Bibles and fragrant oranges.

People he had never seen before, people who had never seen him, were playing a brass band because they were glad he was here! And who was he? William Taylor, collier, from Beggarley Bottom—too poor to pay his own passage over.

A big lump caught in his throat, and he swallowed hard. He shoved his bedroll under one arm. Then, with the other arm reaching out, he ran down the gangway shouting, "Show me your Rocky Mountains!"

III
Some Must Push and Some Must Pull

1

This America had no end. The immigrants had traveled by train thirteen hundred miles from Boston straight across America—and still there was no sign of the Rocky Mountains. For seven days and nights they had watched from dirty, smeared windows as the train sped westward, catching glimpses of America—Albany, Buffalo, Kirtland, Cleveland, and Chicago—all bedecked with red, white, and blue bunting. The conductor called it "Fourth of July."

It would not do, they decided, to miss the Rocky Mountains. Therefore they took turns sleeping against the hard wooden seats. They bounced their fretful babies spotted with heat rash. They shared their jugs of water and divided their dwindling supplies of seafood rations. They propped up the smudgy windows and took turns poking out their heads. What a hot place this Promised Land!

Then, at last, on July 8 the train reached the end of the line. Iowa City, Iowa. End of civilization.

William dropped his bedroll at the side of the station, stretched his arms to the sky, and lifted his face to the summer sun. He had spent his first week in America inside a train rushing past woods and valleys. Now he was ready to run her wide green prairies and scale her highest mountains.

He narrowed his eyes against the sun. It was a magnificent ball of fire. And the sky was endless blue.

He shook his head in disbelief. "Good lawks," he exclaimed. "Good lawks!"

The quiet, dusty streets of Iowa City slowly filled with people—eight hundred and fifty weary travelers teeming from the station, dragging their baggage through town.

"Beyond this place," William shouted, "are the Rocky Mountains." He tossed his cap into the air, kicking up clouds of dust with his heavy boots. "Why, Henry and Jesse and I can—Jesse and I can climb to the tops so fast—"

"Are you ready to escort us now, William?"

He turned and saw his mother sitting on a station bench, Jesse at her side. She was smiling, looking pleased, though her face was flushed red from the magnificent sun.

William walked proudly over to his mother and offered his arm. Then the Taylor family, carrying their bedrolls, began their long walk west.

2

The campground on the bank of the Iowa River was bustling. Fifteen hundred people swarmed on the grassy bottom land, cooking over open fires, washing clothes, and making shelters.

Early in the summer the two Church agents, Elder Spencer and Elder Webb, had outfitted three companies of converts with handcarts and supplies and sent them on their way to the Valley of the Great Salt Lake. But they were totally unprepared for the five hundred additional converts from the ship *Thornton* who had arrived the last of June and for the converts from the ship *Horizon* who were now streaming into camp.

"The letters must have come on the ships with you," Elder Spencer said, shaking his head. "But the Lord willing, we will manage."

"The Lord knew we were coming," Elder Martin said. "He will provide."

"Where are the handcarts?" William asked, looking around.

Elder Spencer pointed to a large tent near the center of camp. Under the faded cover stood rows of unfinished wooden carts, small open boxes on wheels with two shafts extending in front.

"And the others, I'm afraid, are still growing," he said, gesturing to the woods beyond.

William stared in disbelief. These carts were not like Grandfather Taylor's cart that had carried him to Nottingham. They were like the trams in Moorgreen Pit!

"Look you," he gasped, turning to his mother.

His mother nodded. "We are looking, William. We are looking."

Elder Martin put his hand on William's shoulder.

"The Lord will turn you into a carpenter, William," he said. "And your brother into a tent maker." He sighed wearily. "But for tonight, boys, count your blessings and lie down to sleep under the starry vaults of heaven."

The Taylors were joined by the James Stones family, who invited them to share their campfire for the night.

"Have you seen the tinety little carts?" Hannah Rachel asked, as the young people ran ahead of their parents. "They are handcarts—to be pulled by hand."

"We know," William said, provoked that the girls had already explored the big tent. "That should be easy enough."

"We don't ride in them, mind you," Sarah Stones explained. "We pull them or push them. Come, we will show you."

Just then Brother Stones called. "Could you two boys take my hatchet and scout about for some dry wood? I'll walk back to town and see if I can trade anything for food." Then, turning to his wife, he said, "If anyone happens by as looks worse off than we, invite them to stay."

When William and Jesse returned with firewood, the group was much larger. The John Parkinson family, with nine hungry children, had joined, as well as an elderly man called Grandfather Woodcock.

70

The old gentleman sat on his bedroll minding the youngest children. "This must be the Promised Land," he said. "I just saw a butterfly as big as an English song thrush!"

Just before dark Brother Stones returned with a handful of potatoes, and soon there was hot soup for everyone.

In the darkness the campfires of modern Israel flickered brightly up and down the riverbank. Sounds of the soft strumming of fiddles drifted on the warm night air.

Then suddenly, without warning, a thunderstorm struck the Camp of Iowa. Thunder roared, clap upon clap, louder and louder. Lightning flashed ice blue against the sky, and rain fell in torrents.

The frightened campers ran to their tents, but within minutes the tents were ripped from their stakes and whipped away. Water rushed over tents and blankets.

Over and over again the thunder struck. And the lightning flashed. And the wind screeched.

"Mayhappen the Lord is speaking!" someone cried.

"Who could hear above this?" another answered.

William and Jesse huddled together, ducking their heads each time the lightning flashed. During one flash, William noticed a cart from the big tent rolling toward the river.

"Let's fetch it, Jesse," he said. "And sit in it!"

The boys ran after the cart, pulled it back, and braced it in a mud hole. They climbed inside the box with their legs hanging over the edge.

Still the rain fell, but the boys did not care. "I like this tinety little cart," William shouted. He put his arm around his brother. "It's good for sitting in the rain in!"

"Under the starry vaults of heaven!" Jesse shouted in return.

71

"I like this noisy American rain!" William shouted louder.

"So do I!" Jesse yelled.

In the darkness the brothers listened to the voices around them.

"It's the dry climate. Don't worry. Pass the word on."

"It's the dry climate."

"What kind of place is this? Such a dry climate, I have never been so wet!"

"It's the Promised Land."

After a while the thunder and lightning stopped, but the rain continued falling all night.

"Do you think the Lord is chastening us, Jesse? So we will be worthy to enter Zion?" William asked.

Jesse wrinkled his nose, thinking. "Could be, Willy. Could be. But you know, we really needed a good bath."

3

There were things in the Promised Land called chiggers, and they were all over William's legs, biting and stinging. When he tried to brush them off, they crawled on his hands and arms. He sat down on a log to rub his red itching legs. If he could just get out of this long, river-bottom grass—

He looked around the thicket and saw nearby a cottonwood tree with low branches. He struck Brother Stones's hatchet into the trunk and climbed up the tree. Then he took off his boots, tied the laces together, and hung them over a branch.

"Begging your pardon, America," he muttered, "but I don't like your chiggers!"

Moaning loudly, he rubbed his swollen ankles. He would cut firewood later.

Everyone in Camp Iowa was anxious to leave. The passengers from the *Horizon* had been on the riverbank for three weeks, hastily constructing their handcarts. They were now organized as the Saints of the Fifth Handcart Company, with Elder Martin as their captain.

Only a few days ago the five hundred emigrants from the *Thornton*, under the leadership of Captain Willie, had left with their handcarts. Two small wagon trains were almost ready to pull out. Their captains, Brother Hodgett and Brother Hunt, had been instructed to follow the two hand-cart companies.

For three weeks William had carried wood. Logs of hickory and white oak to the sawpit. Oak to the steam box to be bent for wheels. Hickory to the saltwater vat for axles and hubs and spokes. Slabs of any timber left over for boxes and shafts and crossbars. All the timber was green, because there was no time to wait.

Under the big tent the handcarts were hammered together. And each day the line of carts grew longer. This morning William had counted 110 carts. Only a few more days!

He could almost feel the new wooden cart under his hands. He would be so far ahead of the company every morning, Captain Martin would have to ask him to slow down.

He laughed aloud. He knew how to push a handcart. Hadn't he and Henry and Jesse been pushing carts for years? He punched his boots, watching them swing from their laces, and wondered what Henry was doing today.

Suddenly William heard crackling sounds—someone pushing through the underbrush. He held still, not wanting anyone to see him loafing up a tree.

It was Hannah Rachel. Spying on him! Now that the Taylors and Stones were sharing a tent, he was never free from her dark laughing eyes. Every night he found wild flowers on his bedroll—daisies and firepinks. The tent reeked of them. And here she was now, skipping through the woods gathering more smelly flowers. She should be back at camp minding her little brothers.

Hannah Rachel peered around the small opening, then walked over to the tree where William was hiding and looked at the hatchet in the trunk. Her black eyes could see anything!

She looked up into the dense foliage and said calmly, "What are you doing up there, William?"

There was no use pretending he wasn't there now. William dropped down to a low branch, then jumped to the ground.

"Nothing," he said.

Hannah Rachel looked at his swollen ankles. "Gettin' away from the chiggers?"

William slowly put on his boots. "You shouldn't be worrying about chiggers, with a red Indian ahind every tree."

"Red Indians?" Hannah Rachel gasped, and she looked around fearfully.

"Red American Indians. They are just watching now. Watching and waiting."

"For what?" she whispered.

"For the attack. They guard the Rocky Mountains, mind you, in a long line on their horses with their bows and arrows drawn. We have to break through their ranks."

Hannah Rachel stared, frightened. And when a black crow screeched, "Caw, caw," she dropped all her wild flowers and fled, terrified, through the trees.

William rubbed his itching ankles and grinned widely. He guessed he had gotten even with Miss Hannah Rachel.

4

"Slow down, Willy. I'm not pushing back here. I'm just holding on!"

William turned and looked back at his brother at the rear of the handcart. "Just hold on then, Jesse. We don't want Brother Stones to bump into us."

"And I can't see a thing," Jesse hollered. "Except dust!"

The dust of 146 handcarts rose thick and white as the Fifth Handcart Company rolled from Camp Iowa down the narrow stagecoach road that cut through the green prairies of southern Iowa. Under the blazing sun the travelers pushed their screeching, rattling carts through the dust, while their children ran along the roadside and played tag in the long prairie grass.

Mile after mile the converts pushed their noisy carts, singing a gay marching tune. Someone in the long procession would begin singing, and soon everyone would join in, keeping step to the rhythm of "The Handcart Song:"

> *Some must push and some must pull,*
> *As we go marching up the hill;*
> *So merrily on the way we go*
> *Until we reach the valley-O.*

That evening Brother McBride played the same tune on his fiddle for dancing around the campfire.

"How can they dance?" William asked. He was too tired to move even when the campfire smoke blew his way.

Jesse squirmed. "Mayhappen they were just holding on, Willy," he said.

Through the flickering fire the boys watched the members of their tent group, which, including the Taylors, consisted of fourteen people: Brother James Stones, tent captain; his wife, Mary, and their four children—Hannah Rachel, Sarah, John, and James; Widow Housley and her bachelor son, George, framework knitters; George Padley, a young tailor; Sarah Franks, a spinster; and Brother Charles Woodcock, a grandfather.

"Wish Thomas and James Briggs could be in our tent," Jesse whispered. "They would be fun."

"Aye," William answered. "But remember all those crying babies on the ship?"

Jesse nodded.

"They nearly all belonged to Sister Briggs!"

Just then Captain Martin rode up on his white horse to make a night check.

"How many miles the first day, Captain Martin?" William called.

"Seven miles today, son."

"And how many more?" Jesse asked.

"Over a thousand. Over a thousand, easy."

"A thousand miles? A thousand miles left to walk?" Jesse gasped.

"Come on, Jesse," William said in a hushed voice.

The boys hurried into the tent, took off their boots, and crawled into their bedrolls. And when Brother Wadkins sounded taps and their mother came looking for them, they were already sound asleep.

The second day the handcart train traveled nine miles

and camped near a small wood. As soon as tents were pitched, the boys of the camp scattered out to look for firewood.

"Let me take the hatchet, Willy," Jesse coaxed. "I'll find a good log." He pushed through the foliage with the hatchet, and William followed.

"Careful in this undergrowth," William called.

But Jesse had already stumbled. He cried out, "Gosh, Willy, I'm cut!"

William rushed to his brother's side and saw blood gushing from his knee. He grabbed a handful of leaves and pressed them on the wound. Jesse winced.

"Does it hurt bad?" William asked. Jesse nodded.

William took off his shirt and bound it around Jesse's knee. The shirt turned red. "Lean on me," he said. "Let's get back to camp."

Next morning at the shrill call of Brother Wadkin's bugle, Jesse sat up and then tried to stand up.

"Mother," he called. "I can't stand up. I can't walk!"

His mother was at his side quickly. "You may ride in the handcart today, son," she said. "And tomorrow you may feel like walking again."

When Captain Martin shouted, "Fall in," Mary Taylor stepped behind the crossbar of the handcart, and William pushed from behind. But they could not keep up the rapid pace of the other carts, and soon they had to pull off to the side.

The Stones and the Housleys stopped their carts, but Mary waved them on.

"What we need," she said to William, "is something to shade Jesse. I think this sun has given him a fever." She rummaged through the cart for props to hold up a cover, but she could find nothing.

"We may have to wait until we come to some trees," she said, scanning the horizon. "Let's hurry along."

As they were pulling out, they heard a familiar voice singing. "Some must push and some must pull, but I must hobble all the way."

It was Grandfather Woodcock, with two hickory sticks in his hands. Both mornings the old gentleman had started out, with his walking sticks, ahead of the company so he would not be too far behind at night.

"I knew someone would need these," he said, swinging the sticks. "And you do, for sureness. You need a canopy."

He helped Mary and William fasten a cover over the handcart, then continued on his way.

"I'm thinking now of Grandpa Soar," Jesse said, wiping his flushed face with his sleeve. He took a deep breath, trying to ease the pain in his knee.

Slowly the family moved along. The supply wagons loaded with tents and sacks of flour passed, then the small herd of milch cows. By late afternoon the Taylors' handcart was the last cart on the trail.

"I'm sorry, Mother," Jesse babbled as he tossed feverishly. "Causing all this trouble—slowing us down."

"Don't fret about that," she said. "We pray for wisdom, mind you, and God sends us problems to overcome."

"Just a suggestion, Mother," William called from the rear of the cart. "Don't be praying for any more of that wisdom for a while."

5

William pushed against the rickety handcart methodically. Step after step. Mile after mile. Day after day. And Jesse was a ton of coal!

At midday the family approached a small settlement on the old stage road. Farmers in their cornfields were leaning against rail fences, staring after the main company.

"Look you straight ahead, boys," Mary said wearily.

At the far end of the village was a single cabin with an oak tree spreading its branches over the fence, shading the side of the road. Here they stopped to rest. As soon as they stopped, a large man in buckskin stepped out of the cabin and started toward them.

"What do you want here?" he called.

"Just a bit of shade," Mary answered. "We are going now."

"You the last of 'em?" the man asked, looking down the road. Without waiting for an answer he said, "Looks like the lad needs a drink of cold well water."

Mary dropped the crossbar. "That would taste main good to my boy. He's ill."

The man climbed over the fence. "Let me take a look at him."

By this time a woman and three freckled little girls were

peering around the cabin door. The man beckoned to them.

"Fetch some water."

As his wife approached, the man said, "You ought to let my missus take a look at that knee. She uses Indian medicine. Real good at it, too."

Mary gently unwrapped Jesse's bandage. His knee was cold to her touch and swollen beyond its natural size.

"It needs fomenting," the woman said. "Bring him inside." She hurried ahead, the three girls at her heels.

"What's fomenting?" Jesse whispered anxiously as William lifted him out of the cart.

"I don't know," William whispered back. "Just grit your teeth."

Inside the cabin Jesse sat on a bench with his leg propped over a round tin tub. The farmer's wife scurried around the room, mixing herbs and dropping them into buckets of water on the stove. The strange, pungent odors made both Jesse and William sneeze, and that made the little girls giggle.

When the water was warm, William carried the buckets over to the tub as the woman directed. Then he poured the water over Jesse's knee, while the woman added boiling water from the teakettle, making each bucket hotter. Then she wrapped a steaming towel around Jesse's knee.

"Now we'll heat the water again," she said, "and start over."

"Fomenting is carrying water," William said, dropping down on the bench by Jesse.

"Grit your teeth," Jesse said.

All afternoon William carried buckets of water back and forth while the two women nursed Jesse's knee. Finally Jesse began to perspire.

"Good," the woman said, slapping her hands together. "That's a good sign."

She mixed more herbs into a dark thick salve and rubbed it over the white wound. "That's all I can do," she said, "but it will work."

Mary held out her hand to the woman, and their eyes met.

"I would like to give you something," Mary said. "But I have nothing. I pray the Lord will bless you for your goodness to us."

"Doesn't matter," the woman said. She wiped her arm across her own perspiring face.

The farmer came inside with an armload of wood, which he rolled noisily into the woodbox. "If you have to carry that lad all the way to the Rockies," he said, "none of you will make it."

Mary motioned for William to help Jesse to the cart. "Even so, we cannot go be-out him," she said.

"The missus and me could sure use a fine boy around here, come harvest time." The man rubbed the head of a little girl who was wrapping herself around his leg.

"We would be good to him," the woman said excitedly. "We'd see that he got his book learnin' this winter, right along with the girls."

"And if he didn't like it, he could join one of your companies next spring," the man added, pressing closer.

Mary shook her head. "You are kind Christian people," she said. "But we want to go to Zion together."

"My brown mare's just foaled out in the pasture. And I haven't got anyone to give that little colt to. That is, anyone who wants her." The man looked at Jesse and then William.

Still shaking her head, Mary stepped between the shafts of the cart and lifted the crossbar.

"Let's begin of walking, William," she said.

The man followed the Taylor family to his gate. "There ain't nobody ever passed through here this late in the year who ever planned to cross the Rockies. You won't make it. None of you crazy Mormons!"

The woman ran down to the gate calling after Mary. "My man's tellin' the truth. Nobody should be passin' here after June. You won't make it!"

Mary straightened her shoulders and pulled hard. "We are going to!" she said.

The farmer's pasture ran adjacent to the road, and the brown mare and her colt followed along the fence as the Taylors moved down the road. At the end of the pasture the mare stopped, whinnied, and then frisked about with her colt.

"Mother," William called from the rear of the cart, "how can you say that—we will make it—when you have never seen the Rocky Mountains?"

"It's called faith, William. A light inside. A light you know will guide you even when you can't see."

She looked straight ahead as she bent over the crossbar, and William pushed with his eyes shut to avoid the dust. Only Jesse turned his head back to look at the little brown colt kicking and running in the pasture.

6

On the other side of the Missouri River was Indian territory, and as William rode the steam ferryboat across the wide river, he kept a careful watch on the opposite shore. He noticed Hannah Rachel at the front of the ferry, her hands cupped over her eyes, peering anxiously ahead. *Afraid of red Indians,* William thought, grinning.

For four weeks William had pushed his handcart over the rolling green hills of Iowa, through creeks and rivers—Big Bear Creek, Little Bear Creek, North Coon River, Middle Coon River, South Coon River. Four weeks of pushing Jesse up and down hills—and looking for Indians.

"Where are those red Indians?" Thomas Briggs asked daily, trailing his little sisters at the rear of the company. "Just answer me that—where are those red Indians on buffaloes as you were telling about?"

William always answered, "Over the next hill, for sureness."

Now as they ferried the wide Missouri River, William strained to see the opposite shore and the town of Florence, where, Captain Martin said, they would rest a few days.

"Let all the others rest," William said to himself. "But I am going to find work—not pushing anything nor pulling, but work that pays with slabs of bacon!"

Already today he had eaten his food allotment: one pint of milk and one pound of flour. "I'm so hungry," he muttered, "I could eat a buffalo!"

He chewed on a hickory stick and watched the yellow water lapping against the wooden ferry. He also watched Hannah Rachel, brown as her ragged brown dress, searching the Nebraska shore.

"Hold the cart," he whispered to Jesse. Quietly he moved between the handcarts until he stood behind Hannah Rachel.

"Looking for Indians?"

Hannah Rachel jumped straight into the air, her long braids flapping against her back. She whirled around.

"Oh!" she sputtered. "I almost fell in the river!"

William grinned. "Thought mayhappen you were going to jump anyway."

"I was just looking."

"Who for?"

Hannah Rachel looked him squarely in the eye. "My great-grandfather."

William laughed. "I don't believe it."

Hannah Rachel tossed her head, and her braids swished across her back. "Wait and see," she said.

It was so. Waiting on the Nebraska shore were Hannah Rachel's uncle Joseph Stones and her great-grandfather William Stones. They had left England five years earlier, but on their way to Zion they had stopped in Florence.

"I have met every boat this summer," the old gentleman said, "and if you didn't come on the very last one. I have walked nigh on a thousand miles back and forth to this ferry dock every day."

Grandfather Woodcock hugged Grandfather Stones as if they were old friends. "Mayhappen I've found someone as might be able to keep up with me," he told the group, chuckling.

"You haven't heard the talk then?" Joseph Stones asked his brother. "The talk of wintering here in Florence or Wood River—not finishing the trip this year?"

"What's this?" Brother Stones asked.

"You're at least a month late," his brother said soberly. "The Church agents here say as it would be taking a risk to cross the Rockies this late in the season. There might be snow."

"But if there isn't snow?" George Padley asked.

"Then there will be no problem. But it is a risk. I'm staying another season in Florence with my family. We'll go to Zion next spring."

"Except the grandfather," Grandfather Stones added. "If I wait for another spring, mayhappen I shall never get to Zion."

During the afternoon Captain Martin rode his white horse through the scattered tents of the camp, confirming the situation.

"We are over a month late," he said. "Some of the Church officials think we should stay here until spring. The men could find work easily back across the river in Iowa. Talk it over. We will meet tonight."

All afternoon there was talk—but only of moving on.

"The Lord said the top of the mountains, not the Missouri bottoms!" Brother Briggs exclaimed.

That night William, Jesse, and their mother gathered around the big campfire with the other converts, eager to hear the counsel of the Church officials.

A group of thirteen elders returning from England, traveling in horse-drawn carriages, had arrived in Florence the day before. In the group was Franklin D. Richards, the mission president in Liverpool who had arranged the ocean passage for the converts.

Elder Joseph A. Young spoke first. "It is foolish to continue the journey so late in the season," he said. "If it snows, you will lose your lives. My advice is to go into winter quarters now."

The crowd murmured.

"That's what the farmer said, too," William whispered to Jesse. "Remember?"

Jesse nodded.

Elder Richards stepped onto the speaker's platform and lifted his arms. A hush came over the crowd. "The Lord had protected you this far," he said. "He will not forsake you now."

Elder Young raised his arms—and his voice. "The Lord is merciful, my brothers and sisters, but he will not change the elements to suit our every need."

"He held the waters of the Red Sea," a voice shouted.

"We will vote," Elder Richards said. "Each man may decide for himself."

"They cannot vote when they are completely without knowledge of the conditions," Elder Young said adamantly. But his counsel fell unheeded on the zealous crowd.

"We will vote," the voices shouted. "A raise of hands!"

Jesse leaned over to his mother. "How are you going to vote?" he whispered.

Mary put her arm around her boys. "The same Lord as carried us over the treacherous ocean will help us over the mountains." She raised her hand in assent.

"He did do a good job at that," William agreed, nodding to Jesse.

Both boys raised their right hands to be counted.

7

After three days they traveled on, up the north side of the wide, sluggish Platte River, tired from its journey to the Missouri.

"We won't get lost now," Captain Martin said the first night out of Florence. "We'll follow the Platte backward, from the Missouri to its beginning in the top of the Rocky Mountains. "But," he added, "it's a long, long river."

"And that means a long, long walk," William said to his friend Thomas. The two boys stood on top of a sand bluff trying to see the beginning of the muddy river.

"Five hundred miles," Thomas said.

Thomas looked like a different person since William had met him on the ship. He was spotted with brown freckles, and now it seemed as if his skin was curling like his hair.

"And then five hundred more," William added.

The boys stared, spellbound, at this strange American land rolled out under the blazing sun. Endless gray sand. Sand hills twisted into dragons. Tufts of scabby grass, low sagebrush, and prickly pears reaching up through the sand. Buffalo skulls bleaching. Lizards darting.

And cutting through the middle of this gray desert was the muddy Platte River.

"Ever see anything like it?" Thomas asked.

William shook his head. He knew that if he had thought about it all the way from Liverpool, he never could have thought up the Platte Valley. "It's like the Atlantic Ocean," he said solemnly, "all dried up."

"See any red Indians?" Thomas asked, squinting into the horizon.

Again William shook his head. He could not see any Indians, but he knew they were there somewhere, behind one of those bluffs. He heard them at night, and once from a sand bluff he and Thomas had seen the remains of burning wagons. "Cheyenne," Captain Martin had said.

"We know they are out there, William, attacking other wagon trains. Why not us?"

William dropped down on the warm sand. "Could be as we pray all the time as how they won't," he said.

"Another thing," Thomas said, dropping down beside William. "Do you think we will really make it—one thousand more miles of walking and pushing those wobbly carts?"

"It's mostly just walking, Tom. We can walk a thousand miles. We can just keep walking—wherever Zion is."

"Even if it's beyond the Rocky Mountains?"

William nodded. "I been thinking, Tom. I'm not doing all this walking just for a farm—even one with clear streamlets flowing. That's easy to talk about, mind you, but it isn't all. I decided that a long time ago."

William looked his friend in the eye. "We have more than farming to do, Thomas. We are going to help build the kingdom of God on this earth."

"How?"

"I don't know as how because we are not there yet," William said.

"What would you do," Thomas asked, "if the Lord

pointed His finger at this valley and said to build His kingdom here?"

"Right here?"

"Right here on the muddy Platte."

"I guess I'd begin of building a sod cabin, right here on this sand bluff."

"Gollocky, William. And drink muddy water the rest of your life?"

"I'd sift it!"

Thomas had no more questions, and he rolled onto his stomach and contemplated the Platte Valley. In a few minutes he sat up and looked directly at William.

"I been thinking too, William," he said. "I'd like to build my sod cabin right next to yours."

William smiled at his friend. "Thanks, Thomas. I'd like that. But let's hope He doesn't change His mind."

The boys idly watched the handcart caravan at rest, strung out for miles like a tattered ribbon. Soon the carts began moving again, screeching as they were drawn through the soft sand.

William scanned the line. He saw his mother in the blue sunbonnet he had bought for her at Florence. She was pulling between the shafts, and Jesse, limping, was pushing behind. But something was wrong. They were pulling the cart out of the line. William guessed the problem—too much sand in the axle. These days there was always too much sand in the axle!

"Come on, Tom," he said, rising. "We need to get out the bacon rinds again."

Holding on to their caps, the two boys slid down the soft, lumpy hill, dodging prickly pears and scattering the black-eyed lizards.

Inside the dark tent Jesse and William whispered together.

"Do you hear that?" Jesse asked, sitting straight up in his bedroll.

"Aye," William said.

"I think it's wolves," Jesse whispered hoarsely. "They are following our trail."

"It's Indians," William said.

Hannah Rachel bolted straight up in her bedroll. "Indians?" she asked in a trembling voice.

Her sister Sarah bounced up beside her.

"They have been following us since we left the Loup Fork," William said quietly, "whoever they are."

"Why don't we see them in the daytime?" Hannah Rachel whispered.

"They hide ahind trees," William answered.

"But there are no trees about here."

"Then we'll be seeing them afore long. But Hannah Rachel, you better leave the daisies be. You have picked too many in this Nebraska Territory. And the red Indians don't like it."

"Soo, soo, children," Sister Stones whispered from across the tent. "You will wake the little ones. Go to sleep now. The guards will stay awake for you."

William pulled his blanket up over his head, but he did not close his eyes. What would he do when he came face to face with a red Indian?

The Pawnees came without warning, over a sand ridge, like eagles swooping down upon their prey. Mounted on swift, shaggy ponies, they quickly reached the handcart

91

company; then, dividing, they passed single file down each side.

"Be calm!" Lieutenant Tyler shouted, galloping down the line as fast as his old mule would go. "This is not an attack. But be prepared for anything. Keep together!" He kicked his mule and raced back up to the front.

The Taylors pushed hard to catch up with the main body, but the distance was too great, the sand too deep. They leaned against their cart, breathless.

Other stragglers came running, trying to catch up with the Taylors—Grandfather Woodcock, Grandfather Stones, and James Briggs, dragging his three little sisters.

Suddenly William noticed Hannah Rachel, skipping along the wet sand near the river.

"Hannah Rachel," he shouted. "Hannah Rachel!"

Hannah Rachel looked up and saw the Indians. She froze.

"Get back here!" William yelled, waving his arms.

Hannah Rachel stared at the Indians, then William. Suddenly she began running headlong toward the end of the line, yellow daisies clutched in her hands. William and Jesse ran to meet her and, each taking an arm, pulled her back to the cart.

"Get rid of those daisies," William said.

No one knew what to do nor where to look, so they stood still, whispering their fears.

"Pawnees! Thieves! They'll take the weak ones."

William looked at those around him—white-haired grandfathers, frail, tired women, and skinny barefoot children. If only he had a hatchet! And where was Lieutenant Tyler with his gun?

His mother guessed his thoughts. "Don't be afraid, boys," she said, her voice trembling. "The Lord is with us."

92

"I hope He has a gun!" William muttered.

"William!" Mary scolded. Then, seeing the Indians drawing closer, she put her hands over her face and wailed. "Good-dear-a-me. Naked savages. Just like Grandfather Taylor said. This I cannot abear."

The Pawnees flanked both sides of the handcarts, riding easy on their small horses, looking straight ahead. Their brown bodies glistened, and the greased scalplocks on their shaven heads stood up like horns. In their hands they held bows, with arrows fitted to the strings.

William gasped. Like the Platte Valley, he never could have thought up a Pawnee, either. Suddenly a horse on his right came to a stop, and he looked up into the face of a red American Indian.

The Pawnee looked down at William with contempt. Then he exchanged glances with a companion across from him.

William turned cold clear to the ends of his toes. But somehow he recalled words that Captain Martin had repeated many times around the campfire. "Look an Indian in the eye. He has no mercy for weakness."

William did not want to look a Pawnee in the eye. He wanted to hightail it all the way back to the Missouri River. Instead, he nudged Jesse, who was feeling exactly the same way. "Look them in the eye," he said in a raspy voice.

Gathering all his courage, William stepped out in front of his mother and Hannah Rachel and the other Saints. He drew himself up as tall as he could and looked the Indian straight in the eye.

"Hello, red man," he said in a strange deep voice. "Keep moving."

The Pawnee, surprised, glanced across the trail at his comrade, who was being stared in the eye by Jesse. The Indian stared at William for what seemed like forever to the boy. Then he brought his fist up to his bare chest.

"Heap brave," he said. And touching his knees to his pony, he moved on.

For a few minutes after the Pawnees had passed, no one spoke nor moved. Then, like sleepwalkers, the Saints picked up the shafts of their carts and began moving.

Hannah Rachel was the first to speak. "I guess we broke through their ranks, all right," she said, smiling at William. She stuck her daisies in a corner of the Taylors' cart, then joined William at the back and began pushing.

8

A country that could hide its Rocky Mountains for this long was some country! The seven boys soaking their feet in the yellow Platte all agreed.

William and Jesse and their mates Thomas and James Briggs, Johnny and Henry Sermon, and John Griffith lay on their backs, trousers rolled up, caps pulled over their faces. The mid-September sun warmed their bodies while the muddy river water cooled their swollen, blistered feet.

It was Sunday afternoon. They were somewhere on the Platte, somewhere west of the Elkhorn, the Loup Fork, Prairie Creek, Wood River. West of Grand Island and Buffalo Creek. West of the two forks of the Platte.

John Griffith sat up and pulled his feet out of the muddy water. He propped one foot on his knee and examined it for prickly pear slivers. His shoes had worn out weeks ago, and his newly fashioned ones—canvas soles stitched to his stockings—did not keep out the barbed spines of the prickly pears.

"Ow-ow-ow," he squealed, rubbing his sore foot.

The other boys sat up drowsily, regarding John as part of the gray landscape. They watched the water splash gently over their feet. Farther out, the water flowed lazily around strings of sandbars. In the middle of the river was an island of rushes, with snagged driftwood dammed high against the river's current.

Across the wide river (the North Platte, since the river had forked), more sandy plains and bluffs stretched as far as the eye could see. And winding around the bluffs, bending down to the river, was the deeply rutted Oregon Trail.

"The first one to see a Rocky Mountain wins," William announced.

"Wins what?" Thomas asked.

"Wins the game, I reckon."

The boys looked at each other, weighing the idea. They grinned and tossed their caps. It was agreed.

Every day the boys stretched tall on top of their handcarts and perched on the high seats of the supply wagons. Sometimes they raced ahead of the company, climbing the highest sand hills, peering far into the cloudless horizon.

From these high places they saw vast herds of buffalo slowly grazing, and following them, even more slowly through the dry grass, were hungry gray wolves.

They saw valleys of white buffalo bones, bleaching in the sun, where the Indians had driven the huge brown animals over the high bluffs. They saw white alkali patches and dry sloughs, antelope and prairie dogs. And more sand bluffs.

But no mountains.

Captain Martin was consulted.

"So that's what all this racing is about," he shouted good-naturedly from his white horse. "A Rocky Mountain."

He looked off into the distance before he looked back at the boys. "We were three weeks out of Florence at the river forks. And that's about half way to Fort Laramie."

"Three more weeks then?"

He nodded. "Three more weeks."

The boys groaned.

"Three weeks to Fort Laramie," the captain repeated, "about two hundred and fifty miles. But the Rocky Mountains are so tall that you'll see them long before."

Captain Martin saw Lieutenant Tyler beckoning down the line, and he started off at a gallop.

"Look for Laramie Peak," he called back.

Laramie Peak. The Rocky Mountain called Laramie Peak. Who would see it first? The boys ran whooping toward the nearest bluff.

"Come on, mates," Johnny Sermon called one evening as he and Henry dashed past William and Jesse, who were struggling with their tent.

"Can't," Jesse called as the boys ran on. "We have sickness."

For days Brother Stones had been suffering from a sickness that the immigrants called the American Fever. This evening George Padley and George Housley had both taken sick, so William and Jesse were doing double chores.

William looked up from his side of the tent. "There's James, halfway up the butte."

Jesse nodded. "And here we are still setting up tent."

"Can't help sickness," William said. "Remember your knee?"

"I know." Jesse nodded. "But it mads me, just the same!"

The boys were just finishing their work when Grandfather Woodcock and Grandfather Stones walked into camp, carrying their shirts filled with buffalo chips.

"Thank goodness," William said. "Now at least we will have a fire."

"I been figuring," Grandfather Woodcock said, as the group sat eating around their small fire. "If you two boys are going to win that Rocky Mountain game, you need an advance scout—me."

Everyone looked at Grandfather Woodcock, who was too old to climb sand hills. Their tin spoons scooped up porridge in a slow rhythm.

"Mind you," Grandfather Woodcock continued, "I'm not good for much except just plain walking and looking. But my one advantage"—the old man leaned over closer to William and Jesse, and his eyes sparkled—"I start out early. And," he added, rubbing his beard, "I might as well be looking for mountains as just looking."

"For sureness," William said.

"Now, I'll tell you what I will do," the old man continued. "When I see the first Rocky Mountain, I'll whistle three times. You boys drop whatever you are doing and come running afore those other boys are out of their tents. Then you will see it with your own eyes. Now, won't that be fair?"

"Fair, fair enough," William and Jesse both cried.

Grandfather Woodcock chuckled. "Back home in England I was almost blind. Couldn't see a mile from the top of a barn. Now my eyes are so sharp I can stand on one of these buttes and see a hundred miles. Clear as a bell."

"It's the atmosphere," Grandfather Stones said, smiling.

"Well, just spot Laramie Peak," Jesse said, hugging the frail old man. "And whistle loud!"

"There's a place called Fort Laramie," William told the young people huddled together at the evening fire. "It's a

United States military post. We can get buffalo robes and food there."

"But how far to this place?" Sarah Stones asked. She laid a buffalo chip on the small fire and watched it catch flame.

"It better be soon," her brother John wailed.

"It's near Laramie Peak," Jesse said. "We'll be seeing it any day now. Captain Martin said so this morning."

The children heard footfalls and turned to see Grandfather Stones and Grandfather Woodcock coming into camp. Grandfather Woodcock carried his shirt like a sack.

"Come and sit you down," Hannah Rachel said. "And have some porridge."

Grandfather Woodcock shook his head. "Too tired to eat, lass," he said. "I just need to lay me down a while."

At the tent opening Grandfather Woodcock turned. "Almost forgot," he said. "Something good to eat." He tossed his shirt and his penknife.

The children tore open the bundle, then looked up in surprise. "Manna in the wilderness," Grandfather Woodcock said, smiling. "Peel 'em first."

"Manna from heaven," Hannah Rachel whispered.

"Prickly pears!" William frowned.

Hannah Rachel looked up at William. "We cannot lose faith, William," she said. "My father says that is all we have left."

She picked up the penknife and, holding the prickly pears carefully between their sharp spines, began peeling.

William woke early the next morning, thinking of food. He knew all the reasons for the cut in rations—too many people, slow traveling, the thieving Pawnees. He knew, but his stomach did not. He wanted to gather a bunch of those prickly pears before camp broke.

He sat up quickly and bumped his head against the sagging tent, heavy with frost. A white mist sprayed over his head and down his back.

"Ow-w-w-," he squawked.

Across the tent he noticed Grandfather Stones kneeling at Grandfather Woodcock's bedside. Usually both men were gone when he woke.

"What's a-matter?" William whispered.

"My partner has gone off be-out me," Grandfather Stones said, looking helpless as a child.

"What do you mean—gone off be-out you? He's—" William pointed, then hesitated.

The commotion woke the others—Mary and Jesse, the Stones, the Housleys, George Padley, and Sarah Franks. They looked at Grandfather Woodcock, curled up lifeless in his blanket. And then they looked at Grandfather Stones, not knowing what to say.

Finally Brother Stones, who was too ill to get up, whispered, "Someone go for Captain Martin."

Charles Woodcock, age fifty-two, was buried in a sandy grave along the side of the North Platte River, somewhere in Nebraska. There was a brief ceremony. Captain Martin gave a prayer and Brother McBride sang "All Is Well." Then the weary travelers joined Brother McBride singing as they moved onward:

> *And should we die before our journey's through,*
> *Happy day! all is well!*
> *We then are free from toil and sorrow, too;*
> *With the just we shall dwell!*
> *But if our lives are spared again*

100

To see the Saints their rest obtain,
O how we'll make this chorus swell—
All is well! all is well!

William did not sing. He pushed against his handcart angrily and kicked up sand, which blew back into his face, choking him.

"Do you think all is well?" Jesse asked, pushing at his brother's side.

"No," William said. "I feel sore at heart."

"Aye. But, Willy, did you see the smile on his face?" Jesse asked.

"I didn't look."

"Well, he was smiling. Smiling like he was happy to be there. I guess they are singing the song for him—not us."

"That's it, for sureness," William said. "They are singing the song for him."

9

Day after day the camp rolled out upon the endless sand of the Platte Valley. And each day the seven young explorers scanned the barren plains for a Rocky Mountain.

Now in late September the boys began to notice a change in the dry landscape. Perhaps over the next bluff—tomorrow—there would be a Rocky Mountain.

The game brought laughter and hope into camp. If soon there was a Rocky Mountain, then surely soon there was a journey's end. Those who could no longer run cheered the boys on.

"A merry heart doeth good like a medicine," Sister McBride called after them whenever they passed her cart.

Across the river between steep bluffs, a valley of shimmering green appeared, like a garden in the desert. A deeply rutted trail skirted the patches of trees, bending down to touch the water's edge.

The boys consulted Captain Martin.

"It's called Ash Hollow," the captain said, "and that's the Oregon Trail coming down to the river. It's a rest stop for Gentiles. A beautiful spot."

All day, as they moved past Ash Hollow, William kept a look out for a Gentile boy on his way to Oregon. But he saw no one, not even a stray ox.

They passed other bluffs across the river that were

strangely formed—tall and turreted like old English castles. The boys exchanged opinions and decided they must be Pawnee fortifications.

Captain Martin chuckled. "They are called Castle Bluffs," he said. "A curious sight, I will agree. And there are Indians around here, all right. Keep your eyes open, boys."

It was not the boys, however, who saw an Indian, but Hannah Rachel. She was carrying water from the river and sat down to rest under a lone cottonwood tree. When she looked up into the branches, she looked into the face of a withered, sneering Pawnee. She started to run, and then turned and walked back to the tree.

"If you stay there," she bargained, "I will leave you this silver bucket." She set the water bucket down by the tree—and then ran!

Later when Captain Martin explained the tree burial custom of the Pawnee tribe, Hannah Rachel continued to say, "Well, this one was still alive!"

Whatever the condition of the Pawnee in the tree, Hannah Rachel was admired greatly by seven boys in camp.

Daily, from high and precarious places, the boys surveyed the landscape.

"What's that yon?" Thomas asked, pointing into the distance. He was perched on top of a supply wagon.

Appearing through the clouds on the south side of the river was a magnificent conical-shaped rock, towering alone and majestically over the prairie.

"It's a Rocky Mountain!" Jesse shouted, climbing down the wagon.

"Not a mountain," John Griffith said.

"It's a factory chimney," Henry Sermon said.

"Eh, not out here," his brother Johnny scoffed.

"A lighthouse?" James suggested.

"Whatever it is," Thomas complained, "we are on the wrong side of the river."

The boys jumped to the ground.

"Let's go tell Captain Martin there's a lighthouse out here in the desert," William said. And they ran, laughing.

"It's Chimney Rock," the captain said. "I've been looking for it." He raised his binoculars to the west. "It's the halfway marker for Mormon emigrants—halfway between Winter Quarters at Florence and Zion in the Valley of the Great Salt Lake. We'll see it for days. You boys are better than my spyglasses!"

For three days Chimney Rock dominated the horizon. When the caravan arrived across the river from it, Captain Martin and Lieutenant Tyler consulted together.

"Let's cross the river here," Captain Martin said. "I can see the Hodgett wagons have crossed, and I feel certain Captain Willie's company has not gone beyond this point. The river is very shallow here, and the Gentiles won't bother us."

Seven young mates cheered Captain Martin's order. Before anyone could get ahead, they pushed their carts into the muddy water, splashing and yelling. They were first out on the south bank. Now they could explore Chimney Rock!

The boys soon agreed that Chimney Rock was indeed spectacular—a kingly rock to rule over the entire Platte Valley. It was not, however, a Rocky Mountain. It was just a rocky rock. The race was still on.

Another massive rock formation came into view, looming bigger and bigger on the horizon each day. It looked like Castle Bluffs, days back, except it was larger and more frightening. When the boys pushed their wobbling carts between the high walls of Scott's Bluffs, they peered over their shoulders, searching for Pawnees.

Two days up the river John Griffith spotted Laramie Peak. In the early morning, while most of the camp still slept, John ran ahead and climbed to the top of a tall butte. At first he thought it was a cloud, but when the cloud moved away, he saw snow, shining pink, on top of Laramie Peak.

He stumbled down the hill in his awkward canvas shoes, shouting breathlessly, "I saw it! I won! I saw it! Double-down truth!"

William heaved his folded tent into the supply wagon. "Come on, Jesse," he said, grabbing his brother's arm. "Let's begin of moving."

The Briggs brothers and the Sermons were already racing toward the hill. All seven boys met at the bottom.

"I saw it," John cried, waving his thin arms. "Laramie Peak. Thought it was a cloud."

The other boys looked at John Griffith, the skinniest of them all, with admiration.

"Double-down truth," John gasped. He grinned triumphantly.

In one big swoop the boys lifted John to their shoulders and carried him back to camp.

"John Griffith won," they shouted. "Saw Laramie Peak. Thought it was a cloud!"

The Saints cheered. But loudest of all was Sister McBride. " 'Tis hurrah for Johnny Griffith!" she called from her bed atop her handcart. She banged a tin spoon against a skillet. "'Tis hurrah for Johnny Griffith and Laramie Peak!"

The moon hung like a yellow horn lantern in the sky,

giving ample light for William and his friends to hunt prickly pears. William ran ahead, alongside a sand butte, but stopped suddenly when he heard a strange sound.

He motioned for the others to wait.

Moving cautiously around the butte, William saw a white horse tethered to a rock. And then he noticed Captain Martin sitting a short distance away, his head bowed between his hands.

Captain Martin looked up. "Who goes there?"

"I didn't mean to bother you, Captain Martin. It's William."

"Looking for a Rocky Mountain?" the captain asked.

"Sir?" William questioned. "We saw it this morning. John saw it. Remember?"

Captain Martin laughed. "I know." He noticed the other boys then and motioned for them to come and sit by him.

"I want to thank you boys," Captain Martin said as the boys crowded around, "each one of you."

"You do?" Jesse peered into the captain's face.

"You may not realize it," the captain continued, "but you boys have lightened my load. It's lonely being a leader. Did you know that?"

The boys looked at each other, puzzled.

"Where there was misery and discouragement, you boys brought a little laughter—and hope. With your Rocky Mountain game."

"Sister McBride liked it," John Griffith said.

The captain smiled. "You boys have heard plenty of preaching, but I agree with Sister McBride. You are good medicine. And I am grateful to you."

No one spoke for a few minutes. Then William said, "Thanks, Captain Martin. Mayhappen I know what you

106

mean. Tonight I was feeling sorry as Johnny even saw Laramie Peak, because now that the game is over, we are just looking for prickly pears."

"Aye," the other boys said in unison.

Captain Martin grasped William's shoulder and looked deep into his eyes.

"You have realized a great truth," he said, "you and all your mates. It's the journey that counts, not just the last day."

"Like this journey?" Jesse asked.

"Like this journey," Captain Martin said wearily. "This journey started too late, and it has been hindered at every turn. Now, at the end, we face the formidable mountains. We'll need all the faith and strength and good medicine we can muster to cross them."

They sat for a while, listening to the night noises. Then they started back to camp, with Captain Martin leading his mare.

"I been thinking, Captain Martin," William said, taking big strides to keep up with the leader. "About the rest of this journey. We managed that ocean for sureness, and the prairie, and these old sandy plains. And I'd like to say for me and my mates—we can scale those high Rocky Mountains!"

The captain slowed his pace and put his arm around William. "God bless you," he said.

Walking at Captain Martin's side, William felt as tall as the captain himself—in fact, tall enough to swing that bright horn lantern in the sky.

IV
O Ye Mountains High

1

At the beginning of the high country, the swift, clear waters of Laramie River converged with the slow-moving North Platte. Between this fork of the rivers, on the barren gravel flat, stood Fort Laramie.

For twenty-one years this way station had welcomed western travelers—fur traders, gold seekers, and emigrants. All travelers following the Platte River west at came last to the high adobe walls of Fort Laramie.

On October 8, the six hundred weary pilgrims in Captain Martin's Handcart Company dragged themselves and their squeaking carts through the gates of the post. But as Captain Willie's company had discovered eight days earlier, there was no food for sale at Fort Laramie. There were, however, one hundred buffalo robes secured by Elder Richards, and a letter promising wagons of provisions sent to meet them from the Great Salt Lake Valley.

"If they could persist on their way with utmost speed—" Captain Martin read.

"Children of the Lord," Captain Martin cried from the tower steps. "You are hungry, sick, and disappointed, and your carts are sapping your strength as you pull them. But the only hope for us is to move on. The faster we travel, the sooner we will reach the supply wagons from the Valley."

He hesitated, but there was no murmuring.

"You are sorely tried," he continued. "But the Lord's chosen ones must be tried in all things, that they may be prepared to receive the glory that he has for them, even the glory of Zion."

The next day Captain Martin mounted his white horse and led his flock back through the gates of Fort Laramie, tears rolling down his roughened cheeks.

Five hundred miles of towering snowcapped mountains lay ahead.

"We are in the Rocky Mountains, Willy," Jesse said, straining against the handcart where William lay wrapped in a shaggy buffalo hide. "Can you look about?"

William moaned and rolled his head. A fever burned in his head, and his body ached. He wanted to see the Rocky Mountains. He wanted to get out and climb them, but—there were no mountains in Nottingham. And was he not on a journey to Nottingham with Grandfather Taylor?

The fever made him dream. He dreamed he traveled to Nottingham along the side of a wide, rushing river. He could hear it in the night when the cart was quiet. A bitter wind came up, bringing snow, and Grandfather Taylor told him to crawl beneath the bundles of stockings. But during the night the stockings blew away, and he was alone in the old cart—sick and shivering with cold.

"Grandfather Taylor," he cried. "Where are you?"

When William's fever broke, he sat up and looked around. He was alone in the tent. He tried to stand, but his legs buckled beneath him. He was cold, and pains stabbed through his stomach.

He crawled to the tent opening and looked out. The brightness of snow hurt his eyes. He saw Hannah Rachel sitting near a small fire, holding her brothers, all three wrapped in a muddy shawl.

Hannah Rachel looked up, startled. "William," she said.

"I have had a bad dream," William said, crawling closer to the fire. He pulled himself up to a sitting position and looked around at the sagging tents and broken handcarts protruding from the deep snow, at children huddled around small fires.

"What's wrong?" he asked. "Where are we?"

"We are snowed in," Hannah Rachel said with little emotion. "The place is called Red Buttes."

"Where is Mother? And Jesse?" William asked quickly.

"They're out digging up sagebrush for the fire," Hannah Rachel said. "Our tent group is all right, except for Grandfather Stones. He made it through the river at Last Crossing as brave as anyone, though the water nearly knocked him over. But when it began of snowing on the other side, he just sat himself down on a rock and wouldn't move. He died—sitting on the rock."

"Who else?"

"Brother McBride. He carried most of the children across the river. He carried you."

William nodded slowly. "It wasn't a dream then, was it."

Hannah Rachel shook her head. "Here, have some oxhide stew. It tastes bitter, but so does the willow bark." She moved her brothers from her lap and filled a cup with broth for William.

"We burned the buffalo robes," Hannah Rachel continued, "before the river—at a place called Deer Creek. We were told to—" She started to cry. "I wish we had everything back."

113

"Mayhappen that was the reason for the fire," William said, "so everyone would not go back."

"And then," Hannah Rachel said, "when we reached the river, the owner of the toll bridge wouldn't let us cross. So we walked up the river to Last Crossing and waded across. Then it began of snowing—for three days and nights be-out stopping. I thought it would bury us alive."

William stared into the fire. "The hardest part of the journey . . . pushed in the cart . . . carried across the river like a child."

"What?" Hannah Rachel asked.

"Nothing," William mumbled.

Hannah Rachel dried her eyes. "There is something else," she said softly. She reached deep into a pocket and held out her hand which was filled with dried rose berries.

William took the berries eagerly. "Where did you get them?"

"I picked them all along the way," Hannah Rachel said. "We cooked most of them last week. The broth was pink just like wild roses."

"Why didn't you eat these?"

"I was saving them for you."

William smiled. "Eh, thanks. Thanks ever so."

Hannah Rachel rolled a berry around in her palm. "I could hardly stand it—not eating them—when they were right here in my pocket."

"Then why didn't you?"

"I told you. I was saving them for you."

William grinned. "We'll eat them now," he said.

William felt good. He would do something about this snow—immediately.

"Where's Captain Martin?" he asked.

114

"He rides out every day trying to locate the supply wagons from the Valley."

"And we just sit here waiting?"

"We cannot pull the carts through the snow."

"Leave the carts. Begin of walking. Why are we waiting here? Waiting to starve?"

"Only about half of the company is able to walk. The rest have frozen feet or the fever."

William nodded. "I'll go in search of the wagons. I'll get my mates and we'll go out."

He bolted through the snow and fell to his knees. This American snow was like white mud. He stumbled over to one of the paths that crisscrossed the camp. Some women were cooking over a small fire, and he recognized Sister Sermon.

"Where are Henry and Johnny?" William asked.

"Inside." Sister Sermon nodded toward a tent. "They are badly, William."

He opened the tent flap and saw the four Sermon children and their father wrapped in a blanket.

"Come on, mates," he said. "Let's go find the wagons."

When his eyes adjusted to the darkness, William saw the black feet of his friends protruding from the blanket. He looked up helplessly. "I'm main sorry," he whispered. "I'll—I'll report back to you about the wagons."

William trudged along a path, not knowing where he was going, just looking for Jesse. Ahead he saw John Griffith's older sister coming toward him, carrying a stringy sagebrush.

"Maggie," he called, waving.

Margaret walked awkwardly in the narrow path, her feet covered with squares of oxhide.

115

"Hello, Maggie," William said. "I'm looking for John. I thought we could go scouting for the wagons."

Margaret looked down at the scraggly sagebrush. "Johnny was buried yesterday," she said quietly. "My little brother Robby was buried this morning. We will all be dead in a few days."

She stepped around William and shuffled down the path.

William stood staring after her. "John Griffith. Buried yesterday. John Griffith, first to see a Rocky Mountain."

He turned from the path and plunged on into the deep snow. His body ached, but he pressed onward. Outside of camp he came upon a wide path that had been stomped out in the snow. It went only a short distance, but he knew he was going in the right direction. He plunged again into the deep snow and walked and crawled over the drifts, straining to see the mountains through the gray haze. He fell, rested a minute, then forced himself forward.

"Hello, out there," he called. "I am here! Below the Red Buttes. Here. Here. I'm here. William Taylor."

There was no answer. He wiped wet flakes of snow from his face. "Where are you? Where are you, out there?"

William sank down exhausted. His legs could carry him no farther, and his feet stung with pain. "Dear Father," he cried aloud. "What has gone wrong? Where are you?"

He thought of his friends Johnny and Henry sitting in their tent with frozen feet, and he thought of John Griffith, buried yesterday.

"I do not understand," he cried. "Oh, Father, who knoweth all things, I do not understand!"

In the smooth expanse of snow, William noticed the trail of a single horse, and he remembered that Captain Martin had ridden out for help. What was it Captain Martin had told him, before he had the fever? He had said that it was the journey that counted, day by day, not just the last day.

William pounded his fists into the snow. He was cold and hungry and sick to his stomach. And he didn't care what day it was. Maybe Captain Martin did not know so much, after all.

He struggled to his knees and shouted defiantly to the mountains. "Hello, out there. I'm here. William Taylor. Where are you?"

The only sound from the cold, white wilderness was the chilling howl of a mountain wolf.

2

On the ninth day at Red Buttes three men from the Valley rode into camp, leading a small mule loaded with supplies. The men were Elders Joseph A. Young, Daniel W. Jones, and Abraham Garr. They brought news that ten wagons of food and clothing were waiting forty miles west at the mountain pass called Devil's Gate.

The only hope for the handcart company was to move on.

William looked around at the thirteen people in his tent, pallid and spindly, and he wondered if any of them could walk to Devil's Gate. They looked like a collection from a ragman's wagon.

They were all sick—from the American Fever or from Sister Stones' oxhide stew. William had watched Sister Stones make the stew. She boiled a kettle of snow and a strip of hide from a dead ox—and it tasted just like an old boot!

Brother Stones struggled to his feet to organize the group. His broad shoulders lifted the sagging, wet canvas.

"My dear ones," he said. "We have tribulations, but we did not expect a journey be-out problems, even a journey to Zion. Everyone in this tent can still walk, thank the Lord. And if we can walk and push our carts the next few days, we will live."

"I will never make it," Sarah Franks cried, her eyes red from weeping. "I will fall along the way and be eaten by wolves—me, an oddling with no mother or father of my own."

"Nor I," said George Padley from a corner of the tent.

Sister Housley sat with her hands folded in her lap as if she had just finished her last stocking on her knitting machine. "I can push my cart no farther," she said wearily. "Leave me here."

"What has gone wrong? What has gone wrong?" her son George cried. "We have given everything for the new gospel. All of us. Now must we also give our lives?" George was so frail that he gasped for breath after his long speech.

"We must not despair," Brother Stones said, raising his arms. But no one heard him.

Jesse nudged William. "What say, Willy?"

William buried his head between his hands. He had nothing to offer Jesse. He had faced the red Indians. He had eaten oxhide stew. But he could not push that handcart one more mile!

There was a long silence in the tent.

Then William heard his mother's voice, and he looked up. His mother never shouted, but she was shouting now—standing in the middle of the tent, tearing up her blanket, and shouting!

"What's a-matter? What's a-matter?" Her voice rose higher. "I'll tell you what's a-matter! It's snow! American snow. Like the buffalo. Like everything else in this Promised Land. Big!"

"You badly, Mother?" William asked, jumping up.

His mother stared past him, glassy-eyed.

"Don't worry, Mother," William whispered. "Jesse and

I can push a tinety little person like you with no trouble at all."

"We can even carry you," Jesse added.

"I'm not badly, boys," she said, "just stubborn. I didn't come all this way to die outside Zion. I'll walk to the Valley, pushing my handcart. And if I can't walk, I'll crawl!"

She tore the blanket until her hands turned white and tossed the strips to the astonished group. "Tear your last blanket," she shouted. "Wrap your feet, and walk in rags!"

"But, Sister Mary," Sarah exclaimed, "what of the night?"

"If you can't walk today, you will have no need of a cover tonight," Mary answered.

William tore his blanket into strips—as did the others—and wrapped his worn boots. He wound the cloth around and around his boots and up to his knees, tying lumpy knots in the rags. When he stood up, he looked like a goose from Coney Gray Farm.

Hannah Rachel snickered. But when she tried to stand, she toppled over into a pile of rags.

And William laughed.

Undaunted, Hannah Rachel waddled to the center of the tent, lifted her tattered brown dress above her ankles, and danced a clumsy jig. Her sister Sarah grabbed her hand, and together they whirled around the tent, a rainbow of rags.

Then, to William's surprise, Jesse began singing—a song he said he would never sing again—loud like a crow!

> For some must push and some must pull,
> As we go marching up the hill;
> So merrily on the way we go
> Until we reach the valley-O!

Again Brother Stones stood, tears rolling down his gaunt cheeks into his beard. "We'll make it," he said. "We'll make it to Devil's Gate—all of us."

He knelt and held out his arms to the group. "Remember, my children, after many tribulations come great blessings. Now let us kneel together and ask the Giver of all for strength to endure our tribulations."

Peering around the prayer circle, William felt great pride for his mother and for his brother, Jesse. If they could push an old rickety cart to Devil's Gate, he could too!

And for these eleven ragged strangers walking with him—the Stones family, the Housleys, George Padley, and Sarah—he felt a strong bond of devotion.

Hannah Rachel, also peering around, winked at William.

William grinned, then bowed his head. That Hannah Rachel was some girl!

As Brother Stones raised his voice in prayer, William added his own. "Remember all those prayers about me— William Taylor? Well, it is not just me, but all of us here together."

3

The Sweetwater River, thrashing its way to the North Platte, had carved a deep gorge through the Rattlesnake Mountains. Only the river passed through the craggy gorge of Devil's Gate. All travelers circled to the south, descending to a sagebrush plain level with the river.

The fires at Devil's Gate camp burned night and day, leaping high into the sky. They cheered the hearts of all those who rounded the mountain—first Captain Martin's handcart company, then the Hodgett and the Hunt wagons. Altogether about twelve hundred Saints swarmed around the huge fires.

"This is the hottest place on earth," William said, moving away from the fire. His long black coat, issued from one of the Valley wagons, trailed on the snow.

"And the coldest," Hannah Rachel mumbled through her scarf. She moved toward the fire.

"What I want to know," Jesse said, taking a deep breath and blowing it out, "is now that we are in the Rocky Mountains, will we always see our breath white on the air?"

"Don't know about that, Jesse," William said. "But I have never seen fires so big as how you can't stand close enough to get warm!"

George Padley, who had been hauling cedar trees all

morning, rushed over to the campfire. "The captain says it's time to move on," he called. "Across the river. Away from this windy flat and closer to timber. Until more wagons come."

"Across that river?" Sister Housley asked. She began to cry.

"One more should not matter, Harriet," Mary Taylor said, putting her arm around frail Widow Housley. "We made it here when we thought all was hopeless."

"But it wasn't then when we thought it was, but mayhappen it is now when we think it isn't," Sister Housley cried.

"Good-dear-a-me," Mary gasped, raising her hands in exasperation. "Good-dear-a-me!"

William pulled his handcart through the frozen willows to the steep bank of the Sweetwater, then stared down at the river and the ice whirling like broken glass.

Up and down the riverbank, handcart pilgrims were staring at the turbulent water. Then, shaking their heads, they turned their carts back.

"We will wait here for the wagons," they murmured.

William looked toward Brother Stones and saw him bending over his cart. It was the fever again. He would be no help in crossing the river, William knew.

"He's badly again," Sister Stones cried, rushing to her husband's side. "Oh, James," she wailed, "how will we ever cross this river be-out you?"

As the crowd backed away from the river, three young men from the Valley stepped out in front. Even in their bulky sheepskin coats, William could tell they were not much older than he was.

"We'll carry each one of you across," one of them shouted. "And you won't get very wet either."

"Well, what say, William?" Hannah Rachel looked up at him.

William turned his head and gave his cart a swift kick. Then he gritted his teeth and grabbed the crossbar so hard the old cart rattled. He had been carried across the last river like a child, and no one was going to carry him across this one!

"Let's begin of moving," he shouted, pulling the cart down the steep bank. "Fast, so we can be the first ones on the other side!"

Hannah Rachel and Jesse had to run to catch the back of the cart.

During the night a wind came down the granite mountain, screeching around the cove like a wild beast, snared. It devoured every fire and leveled every tent.

"I thought there wasn't any wind in this place," Sarah Franks shrieked under the collapsed tent. "I have never heard such a racket."

"You're the racket, Sarah," George Padley shouted. "Stop screaming and crawl out."

The night was filled with confusion. Tents and bedrolls were whipped away by the wind, while people ran after them blindly.

William and George crawled through the snow, searching for their handcarts. They found the Taylors' cart a short distance away, its crossbar buried in a snowdrift.

"You rickety old thing," William whispered, tugging at the cart. "All that pushin' and pullin' and complainin'. But you are worth every mile tonight."

They dragged the cart back to the tent and turned it on its side. Then, pulling the heavy canvas over it, they made a small shelter.

"We'll wrap this tent around us like a big blanket," George said, "and hold on."

"Crawl inside," William shouted to the bewildered group.

Snow came on the wind, circling the mountain cove with a white fury. As the storm raged, William heard a voice from a shelter nearby—a familiar voice, wailing and talking.

"That you, Tom Briggs?" he called.

There was a pause. "Aye. That you, William?"

"Aye. That you talking to yourself?"

"Talking some. Praying some. I'm holding down our tent."

"Same here."

"Well, somebody has to be end boy on a flapping tent."

"For sureness."

"William."

"What, Tom?"

"I don't think I am going to make it."

William hesitated, not knowing how to answer his friend. And when he did, he sounded much braver than he felt.

"You have to make it, Tom. This night won't last long. It's just one of those nights as takes a lot of faith—and that good medicine. Remember?"

"Aye."

"Remember our talk on top of the sand butte about mostly just walking?"

"Aye."

"Well, just talk and pray, Tom. And hold on!"

William woke with a jerk, and for a minute he could not

believe he had been asleep. When had he stopped talking to Thomas?

The storm had subsided, and only thin strings of snow continued to fall. A crackling cold light filled the granite cove. William stuck his head out of the canvas. "Briggs," he called softly. "Tom Briggs."

There was no answer. William called again. "Thomas Briggs."

Still there was no answer. William supposed that Thomas Briggs, end boy on his tent, had also fallen asleep.

4

"Up haw! Up haw! Rock and roller. Pull together now."

The shouts of the teamsters filled the frosty morning air as they urged their oxen up the steep incline of Little Mountain, the high entrance into Emigration Canyon.

William moved to the front of the wagon and peered out. He did not need to look out to know that they were going up a mountain, but someone had said this was the last mountain, and he hoped maybe he could see something besides white snow and white wagon tops.

Outside, deep banks of snow flanked both sides of the trail. A long line of wagons trailed behind, and a long line moved vanward. Ahead of the wagons, teams of horses were breaking and packing the snow into a trail. And in front of the horses, barely visible to William, a brigade of men was lined to the top of the mountain, shoveling through drifts of snow taller than the Conestoga wagons.

It looked the same, yet William knew it was different. He could tell by the merriment of the Valley men that it was the last mountain.

A Valley man rode by on his horse, shouting. "All those who can, jump out and walk behind the wagons! It will help the oxen!"

Jesse and the Stones children were already climbing

over the back of the wagon, jumping down as they had done many times during the past weeks.

"It's the last mountain, children," Sister Stones called after them.

From the wagon ledge, Mary waved to a teamster driving oxen. "Bear a hand, Brother. I'll be walking now into Zion."

"But, Sister—" He looked at her bandaged feet.

"Good-dear-a-me," Mary exclaimed, reaching out. "A few more miles won't matter to these feet!"

The other passengers crowded to the front to look out. They looked like strangers to William. They wore other people's capes and coats, and their hands and feet were wrapped in bandages. He looked away, but he still remembered.

He remembered that long cold night in the mountain cove on the Sweetwater when he and George Padley had held down their tent. During the darkness of that night death had visited every tent in the camp. In the Stones' tent, George Padley, nineteen years, holding down his end of the tent. In the Parkinson tent—the family remembered from Camp Iowa—Brother and Sister Parkinson; Joseph, sixteen; Mary, three; Esther, two; and baby William. In the Sermon tent, Brother Joseph Sermon, his arms circled around his boys. In the Briggs tent, Brother John Briggs; Mary Briggs, seven years; and Thomas, thirteen, holding down his end of the tent.

William did not remember the names of all the others— one-third of the company. But he remembered their faces. He would remember them always, as he would also remember the sound of Captain Martin's rifle firing into the air to keep the wolves away.

After three days, they had left the mountain cove, with

128

the sick and infirm crowded into the Hodgett wagons, whose heavy freight had been cached at Devil's Gate.

As the wagons lumbered across the frozen Sweetwater River, William had looked back at his handcart, abandoned in the cove. He watched it become smaller and smaller until it was just a dark spot in the snow.

The caravan had climbed slowly, following the Sweetwater to South Pass, the high ridge that divides the continent. Along the trail they had met men and supply wagons from the Valley, waiting to carry them onward.

Up high mountains and down deep canyons the wagons had moved forward. To Fort Bridger on Black's Fork. Through Echo Canyon, where the shouting of the men resounded against the red sandstone walls. Down Weber and East canyons. Up Big Mountain, where the snow lay twenty-five feet deep. And now, on the last day of November, Little Mountain—the last mountain.

"This is the last mountain," William said, as if trying to believe it himself. He leaned out the front of the wagon with the others, straining to see the first view of the Valley of Promise.

Soon the heavy, creaking wagon jolted over the crest of Little Mountain and leveled out.

"Look you," Sister Stones exclaimed.

Through an opening in the rugged canyon, William saw the Valley of the Great Salt Lake—snow-covered, shimmering white under the blazing sun, protected on all sides by towering silver mountains.

Big, William thought. Big. And even from this brief mountain view, he could see there was plenty of room in that valley for building up!

"Hurrah, hurrah!" everyone shouted. "Hurrah for Zion!"

Unable to contain his joy, William leaned far out of the wagon and reached upward. "I'm here," he shouted. "Right on top of your mountains!"

A horse and rider approached on the packed snow.

"If you are going to jump out of that wagon, William," Captain Martin called, "hop on!"

William slid along the wagon seat and reached out to the captain. Rolled in bandages, his hands and feet looked like balls of snow.

Captain Martin leaned over and, in one big swoop, lifted William up behind him. Then, with a flash of the reins, the white horse galloped over the snow, passing the wagons, the horse teams, and the brigade of men.

Soon everyone was left behind, and it seemed to William that no one else was in the deep, white canyon except the two of them racing under the clear blue sky, splashing through clear streamlets, just as the missionary had said so long ago. And as his thoughts returned to Beggarley Bottom, he wondered what Grandfather Taylor would say about a horse like this!

The swift ride down the canyon left William breathless, and when the horse slowed to an easy gait, there was a long silence. William wondered if Captain Martin had forgotten him on the back.

"I guess this is the last day of our journey," he said, peering around Captain Martin's broad back.

"It's the last day of this journey," Captain Martin replied over his shoulder, "but tomorrow begins another one."

"Another one?"

"Another journey of laughter and sorrow." Captain Martin's voice was melancholy. "And looking for mountains. Much like the journey you have just taken."

"Aye," William replied, though he did not understand the captain right away.

"This has been the most difficult journey of my life," Captain Martin continued. "And my heart is heavy. It may be your hardest journey too, William. So early in your life— so late in mine. But I don't suppose that matters much, in the long run."

"Aye," William said.

"You have journeyed bravely, William," Captain Martin said. "And that's really all that matters."

"Thanks, Captain Martin," William replied. "It was mostly just walking."

At the mouth of the canyon the horse stopped, and Captain Martin did not urge him on. On both sides of the canyon, gentle foothills rolled down from the towering mountains, rippling with mounds of snow.

Buffalo under there, William thought. *Or in this Land of Promise it could be cabbages.*

The Valley lay below—vast and white and beautiful. William felt he could almost reach out and touch the small adobe and brick houses, laid out neatly in blocks, with smoke curling up from their chimneys. Somewhere in this valley, he knew, there was a place for him—for his adobe house and his cabbage farm. Here he would labor all his days to build up the kingdom of God.

William heard a dog bark and jingling of bells. In the distance he saw a horse-drawn sleigh following a creek toward the canyon. The sleigh was crowded with people waving and calling. They were coming to welcome the homeless Saints—to welcome him, William Taylor from Beggarley Bottom—to Zion.

William swallowed hard.

"I been thinking," he said abruptly, but then he became

silent, trying to put his feelings into words. He had been thinking for three weeks in the infirmary wagon, where there was plenty of time for thinking, about those bitter sorrows and those unexpected joys Captain Martin talked about. And he'd been asking over and over: Why?

Now, as he wondered what he could say to Captain Martin, he realized that he did not need to understand everything. He just needed to meet each day with courage. Wasn't that what Captain Martin had been telling him?

William drew himself up tall behind the captain. His heart was pounding until he thought his chest would burst—longing for yesterday, singing for tomorrow. It was a good day for ending a journey.

"What were you going to say, William?" Captain Martin asked, turning around. His kind blue eyes were tearful.

"I was going to say," William replied, holding fast to the captain's coat, "tell this white horse—let's begin of moving!"

Author's Note

Show Me Your Rocky Mountains! is based on a true story. William Henry Taylor was born January 22, 1844, near Eastwood, Nottingham, England. He was one of two thousand European converts to The Church of Jesus Christ of Latter-day Saints who emigrated to America in the year 1856 and pushed a handcart to the Valley of the Great Salt Lake. He was twelve years old. Although he survived the journey, he died July 3, 1860, in Payson, Utah, at the age of sixteen from the recurrent American Fever.